Truth

Robbie Dorman

For Christina and Grandma.

1

"Welcome, once again, to The Truth! I'm Leo Price. Let's get to it."

Leo's piercing green eyes stared into the camera for a moment, letting a brief welcoming smile fade into a practiced, confident gaze.

"The conflict in Israel has escalated, with both sides now utilizing chemical weapons," said Leo, the shot of him at his news desk cutting to chaos on the streets of Jerusalem. Harried men, women, and children are running through clouds of white vapor, everyone shouting and screaming, with gunshots heard in the background.

"Our President has condemned the behavior of the Palestinians, who started the barrage early this morning, instigating the Israeli response in kind," said Leo.

The camera cuts to the President, hair flopping as he nods his head as he speaks, emphasizing every word.

"We cannot, and will not, accept these violent efforts by Palestine. The United States will take all possible action to support and defend her allies, and that includes aerial strikes."

The camera cuts back to Leo, his dark blond hair firmly in place.

"Strong words from our President, but ones that are sorely needed. For too long we've played softball with these countries, and for once, an iron fist might be what is required."

Another camera cut and Leo turns to face it, as they move onto the next segment.

"In other news, NBA player Morgan Johnson ignited a firestorm of controversy when he turned his back during the national anthem during last night's playoff match-up against the Pistons. He was outspoken afterward, criticizing the government's recent policy change against illegal immigrants," said Leo, a video of the game playing, Johnson's back turned as everyone else faced the flag and anthem singer, and then of him answering questions in the locker room.

"There has already been a response from the Pistons owner, Ted Bravura," said Leo, and the camera cuts to him standing at a podium.

"This is a travesty," said Bravura. "This is the playoffs, the most exciting time for basketball fans, and Johnson has to commit such a selfish act. Our country deserves our unwavering support, and this blatant attention grab is shameful and doesn't belong in our organization. I have demanded a response from the league office."

"Strong words from a strong man," said Leo. "Men paid millions of dollars to play a game, and they still can't be satisfied. Embarrassing. The flag merits respect."

The camera cuts back to Leo. "Before we continue, a word from our sponsor."

A prerecorded video plays, with Leo now sitting in his home office. He's typing at his computer. He turns to face the camera.

"I'm no stranger to late nights and long days, as I try and break the latest story, or get in touch with sources across the globe. When I'm feeling run down, or need a burst of energy to keep me working hard, I reach for Dynamite Energy Formula, the newest and best energy shot from our friends over at Blasco."

He reaches for the small bottle and holds it up to the camera.

"Dynamite Energy Formula packs vitamins, minerals, and nutrients into a two-ounce shot that will keep you awake and active throughout the day while giving your body everything it needs."

Leo downs it and smiles, and then puts it down and gets back to work.

The feed cuts to Leo at his news desk.

"Thank you again to Blasco and Dynamite Energy Formula for sponsoring and supporting the program. It wouldn't be possible without you," said Leo.

"Now, I want to show you folks at home a worrying trend I was alerted to by a viewer in Montana. I flew out there personally, and I was alarmed by what I saw," said Leo, and the feed cuts to an establishing shot of a ranch. Rolling hills and forests flash across the screen before showing Leo walking with a middle-aged man in a flannel shirt and blue jeans, wearing a cowboy hat, boots, and sporting a gigantic mustache.

"This is Woody Johnson, owner and proprietor of Johnson ranch, a little bit outside of Great Falls, Montana. Johnson is an honest, hard-working man, and he invited me to his land after he noticed a worrying trend, one that I think deserves attention and investigation," said Leo's voice over, as they walk together through Johnson's land. Johnson is about six inches taller than Leo, but Leo's shoulders are wider. Leo is dressed similarly to Johnson.

"We've got some awful wildfires lately," said Johnson, now recorded as they go. "Just awful. The past few years have been dry as a bone. Been threatening our cattle."

"Have you lost any?" asked Leo.

"Not a one," said Johnson. "We been lucky about that, but we've had some close calls. But it ain't the fires that had me call you out here."

"Then what was it?" asked Leo.

"Just you follow me," said Johnson.

The feed cuts to a blackened forest, Johnson and Leo stepping between charred, broken trees, the ground dark with soot and ash. Leo grabs a piece of char off a nearby tree and rubs it between his fingers, turning them black.

"This is part of our land that got hit by the fires," said Johnson.

"Looks recent," said Leo.

"That's what you'd expect," said Johnson. "But this fire burnt three years ago, put out by them choppers that drop chemicals on the fires."

"Fire retardants, suppressants," said Leo. "Right?"

"That's what they say," said Johnson. "But I got a question for you."

"Shoot," said Leo, as they stood in the desolate woodland.

"How long do you think it takes for a burnt forest to start growing again?" asked Johnson.

"Oh, I don't know," said Leo. "I imagine if the fire's gone, it shouldn't take too long."

"Less than a year," said Johnson. "Most forests see growth again a year later. Or theys supposed to. Not here."

"Why do you think that is?" asked Leo.

"The only reason I can suppose is them chemicals," said Johnson. "Whatever it is they dropped on the forest, not only did it put out the fire, it also killed everything, deep down into the dirt. Only thing makes sense why it ain't growing back."

"That's scary," said Leo.

"You're telling me," said Johnson. "This land is how I make my living. The fact that somebody would want to kill it is terrifying. But that ain't the worst part."

"What could be worse than that?" asked Leo, still rubbing the soot between his fingers.

"The why, Leo," said Johnson. "Why would they do this? Not just here, but all over the place. There's more and more wildfires, I see them all the time in the news. And they're dropping these chemicals everywhere, all over the country, killing the land. Why would they be doing this, if they're not preparing for something?"

The feed cuts back to the same establishing shot, with ominous music playing now.

"Why indeed?" asked Leo, back at the desk. "Tune in tomorrow as I investigate the local Montana officials, and ask the tough questions about fire suppression chemicals."

He turned, facing the second camera. "And now, senior reporter John Stahlbock."

The feed cuts to John Stahlbock, who's at a different news desk, smaller than Leo's, but in the same style. He smiles, handsome, teeth gleaming, eyes honest.

"Thanks, Leo. Today, I wanted to feature something we don't see enough of these days, and that's good intentioned hard work, without excuses."

The feed cuts to a street, with well-manicured lawns, and beautiful, clean two-story houses. It pans out, and then cuts to a little girl, blond hair, sitting at a lemonade stand, smiling for the camera.

John's voice intrudes. "Meet Elizabeth Borne, though she prefers to go by Libby. She's an All-American girl. She's an Honor Roll student and a cheerleader for her brother Ronnie's pee wee football team. But then tragedy struck."

"We were playing in the yard when Scruffy ran out into the street. Ronnie chased after him, and then, and then the truck hit Ronnie," said Libby, for the camera.

John's voice again. "Ronnie suffered a broken leg, saving his dog in the process. But the Borne family has had a tough time lately, with Steve Borne, father of the household, losing his long-held position in the town's textile factory, and with it, their insurance. Faced with medical bills, Libby didn't complain. She went to work."

"My papa always told me that winners work hard," she said. "So I opened up the lemonade stand to help pay for Ronnie's leg."

The camera cuts to people gathered around her table, buying cups of lemonade, including a group of firemen, their big truck parked nearby.

"Libby started her lemonade stand, and it was an instant success. Her effort and dedication inspired others to show support, most notably their local firefighters. Now Ronnie's leg is paid off, and Libby is continuing to work while her dad tries to get back on his feet."

The feed cuts to him, standing behind her in their front lawn. "She's such a good little girl, and she makes me proud. We need more kids like her in the world."

The camera cuts back to John, at his desk once again. "Couldn't say it better myself. Back to you, Leo."

"Thanks, John, for that lovely look at little Libby Borne," said Leo, smiling. "We're just about done here today, but before we go, it's time for some straight shooting."

The camera cuts again, with Leo facing the camera head-on.

"The term fake news is thrown around a lot lately. So many bleeding hearts and snowflake liberals crying out, fake news, fake news, whenever something comes out that doesn't fit their worldview. They attack me, they attack this show, because I try and present an alternative, something outside of the monopolized, commoditized, pasteurized for your consumption mainstream media."

He paused. "Which is what you deserve. You deserve unfiltered, unprocessed news, delivered to you, for you to decide on, for you to understand. Every day, more and more people are deciding what you see and hear long before it gets to you. And this is my promise, this is my pledge, that I will fight with all my power and being to give you the unfettered access you deserve. My only request is that when you hear fake news, you look long and hard at who's shouting it."

They cut back to the other camera, and Leo turns to it. "That's it for us today. Thanks for watching, and don't forget that this is The Truth!"

Credits roll and Leo gathers his notes, and then they're done for today.

"Great show, Leo," said John, as Leo left the news desk, making way toward his office. John walked in step with him, as cameramen and crew segued toward their next task.

"Thanks, John," said Leo. "Good work yourself, on that lemonade stand piece." Leo let a small dose of bitterness through. He couldn't help it. The whole goddamn show would be lemonade stands if John got his way.

John smiled straight through his sarcasm. If John recognized it, he didn't betray it. "Thanks! I was wondering if we could talk, Leo, about the direction of the show. Privately, I mean."

They continued to walk down the long hallway that led to Leo's office. Warren would be joining him there shortly for their post-show discussion, and then Leo would go home for the day. He didn't have time for this.

"What's wrong with the current direction?" asked Leo.

"Oh, nothing's wrong with it," said John. "I was just wondering if maybe we should be going further with our stories. Do they need to see another piece about the president? They're bombarded by that stuff all day."

"We're not giving them the news, John," said Leo. "We're telling them how to feel about the news. We're telling them what's good and bad. We help them make sense out of their lives. We assure them their feelings are valid."

"Viewer surveys have—" said John, but Leo cut him off.

"I know," said Leo. "They want comfort food, they want lemonade stands. But that's only what they say, John. You can't trust them. They don't know what they want. You do good work here, and you fulfill a role. I need to talk to Warren. I'll see you tomorrow."

Leo left John in the hallway. John wanted his position, wanted the show. Everyone knew it. If he was trying to hide his ambition, he was doing a piss poor job of it. Leo would cut him off at the knees every chance he had. If John expected otherwise, then he was dumber than Leo thought.

John had all the tools. He was handsome, and tall, and spoke with conviction. But he was no Leo Price, and they both knew it. That damned pretty boy wasn't taking his spot. Not while Leo still had his balls.

He closed his office door behind him, the thick oak sealing off the noise from the studio, and he let the silence envelop him. He got so little of it. He poured himself a finger of bourbon and waited with it at his desk for Warren.

Five minutes later, Warren Miller knocked three times and then came in. He didn't look his sixty-three. He was still the dynamo that Leo had met a decade earlier. Bald with glasses and a white goatee, Warren was dressed in the same simple slacks and dress shirt he wore every day.

"Good show today, Leo," said Warren, looking down at his clipboard. He paced in front of Leo's desk, never bringing up his gaze.

"Word from El Capitan is to tread lightly on the Israel stuff," said Warren.

"What more does he want?" asked Leo. "He's stomping on people's flowers and I'm giving him a foot massage after.

He should be on his hands and knees, thanking me. I'm the only reason anyone still likes him."

"Hey, you don't have to hear it," said Warren. "We get preference for inside info, ok, so I say yes, thank you, sir, and we keep getting it. Speaking of, there's something supposedly big coming down the pipeline, and if we catch wind of it, we ignore it."

"Something big, and we ignore it?" asked Leo.

"Word is we won't even hear about it if everything goes to plan," said Warren. "Outside of our purview, I was told anyway."

Leo sighed. "I'll just keep my head in the sand and let everyone else get the fucking ratings, then, huh?"

"I know, I know," said Warren. "We'll be fine. I got some good stuff from a border sheriff in Texas, about drug cartels."

"Real?" asked Leo.

Warren looked at him finally, and shrugged with his face. "Real enough. Heartbreaker of a story."

"Sounds great then," said Leo. "On location?"

"One day shoot," said Warren. "Get you in on Saturday, be home by Sunday night."

"I'd like a weekend at some point, Warren," said Leo. His bourbon was gone.

"I could always send John. He'd be more than happy—"

No, no, no," said Leo. "You're not sending that rat fuck on my stories. He can go mine another lemonade stand."

"Don't know why you treat him like that," said Warren.

"Don't give me that shit," said Leo. "I know he wants my job. Hell, he'd take yours if it wasn't so much goddamn work."

"He just wants some input. And he'd probably make your life a little bit easier if you let him."

"Yeah, it'd be way easier when I'm sitting at home, unemployed," said Leo. "He wants to turn the show into a goddamn joke."

Warren didn't say anything to that, flipping through his clipboard. "You staying tonight?" he asked, finally.

"I need a break," said Leo. "We can plan next week tomorrow."

Leo's house was warm when he got home.

"Goddamn AC," he said, cursing at the box as he fiddled with it. He had spent a fortune on repairs, and it still didn't work.

He sat down, poured himself a bourbon, and drank it as he watched The Truth. It was a good show, even John's lemonade stand segment. It was the highest rated show on the network. Leo had the top Q rating of any of their hosts, whatever that was worth.

"Not goddamn bad," he said, into his bourbon. He flipped to the other news channels. Needed to know the competition. Warren told him that. Was John watching them? No, he was probably plowing whatever model he was dating this week.

His phone buzzed next to him, and he looked, a text message from one of his sources, a cyber-intelligence consultant that worked somewhere in DC. Given him some good stuff before. But it usually only came in emails. He called himself Bl@ck H@t. Leo let him have the dumb name.

Got something big

Leo texted back. *Email me details. I'll check it out.*

Too big for email. Can't leave digital trail

Too big for email? Warren's words repeated in his head. "Something big coming down the pipeline."

Leo ignored his thought, texted back. *When do you want to meet?*

Now was the response, immediately.

He had just gotten home, and traffic was going to be a pain in the ass. But the idea did thrill a part of him. Meeting a source in the dark. Like a proper journalist.

That big?

The ellipses bubble appeared and then disappeared, appeared again. Black Hat was hemming and hawing. Leo was about to pour himself another bourbon when he finally received his response.

This will destroy lives

Leo put down his bourbon and set up the meeting.

2

Leo drove to Wal-Mart in the dark. Leo didn't know what to expect from the meeting, but there was a feeling arcing in his guts, a particular anxiety he hadn't felt in a long while.

The traffic was gone by the time he left his house, the commuters having gotten home, the roads now mostly deserted. Black Hat insisted on Wal-Mart, and I guess it made a certain sense. No one gives a shit about what happens at Wal-Mart.

The window was down on Leo's truck, the warm summer air whipping through the cabin. He used to not have the choice. His and Diana's blue sedan didn't have working AC and the summers were always brutal. They had bought a new car when the first break came, when the expose on the chemical dumping broke, and they were suddenly both in high demand.

There had been a lot of late night meets then. The factory was leaking like a sieve. The line workers were getting cold feet when they heard about the cancer, the stillbirths, the deformities. Every time it was a thrill. Not like in the movies, but close enough. Flashlights, darkness, meeting in abandoned lots and parking garages and shitty motels. The nerves were there, the arc of electricity that made Leo's hands shake. They shook because there were consequences, for them and the whistleblowers. Consequences for revealing the truth.

The rest of the work was easy, boring by comparison. It was sitting at a desk and pumping out the words. Leading the reader from point to point, building your report. It was construction. This was espionage. Wetwork.

Everything had changed with their names out there. The couple hadn't had to hunt down sources anymore. Informants piled up at their feet, asking for help and to be relieved of guilty consciences. They all wanted their story to reach the people.

Diana had always hated it. The construction was the thrill for her. The justice of truth, the condemnation of the cover-up, the punishment of the unreachable, all realized by putting type to print. A class action suit sprang up overnight after their piece ran and the company paid out billions. Leo and Diana moved on, unearthing the next scandal.

Eventually, Diana had stopped coming on the meets altogether. The nervousness, the arc, the anxiety, it got to her too much. She couldn't sleep afterward. Leo would sleep like a baby, the only time he ever did.

Leo thought back, the humid summer air swirling

around him.

It had been seventeen years since his last writing gig. Well, last serious writing gig. He still wrote opinion pieces for whatever outlet would pay him now, but they were fluff, unarticulated ramblings cobbled together from an hour's research. More read them than any of his real journalism.

Fuck. Seventeen years? Diana had been gone by then. He had left the paper, and she saw it as leaving *her*. It was already getting worse then, and he wasn't going to starve while he busted his ass. After busting his ass for *years*. Television was the future, hell, video was the future. Who the fuck was going to *read* the news? Joe Armchair didn't prop up a newspaper anymore. He turned on the TV. Or looked at his phone. And they thought a bigger lifestyle section would fix that. Fucking idiots.

Black Hat had texted him out of nowhere then, an unknown number, three hours into a good drunk.

Big fan, got some info for your show if you want it

Leo texted him back. Turns out the tip was solid. Black Hat sent him an email with some dirt on a congressman that Leo spun into one of the few stories on The Truth that had a basis in actual fact. It won him some positive press, for once.

None of the information that Black Hat would leak him over the next few years would ever equal that initial dump. Still, it was worthwhile. It was free. BH didn't even ask for an autograph.

Seeing my info on your show is worth it, really satisfying to see I helped

Feels cool to be a real life informant, lol

Let me know if I can help

Leo didn't know why he had texted Black Hat out of the

blue one day, sitting at home, watching The Truth, but he did.

You watching?

The response was immediate.

Of course, I never miss it

Leo had talked him through the production, giving him details about each segment. BH ate it up. This continued for a while. It led to messages about other things, about other shows, other news, and finally about life. One day Leo realized that he was developing a friendship with this man, that he had never met, that had leaked him information dozens of times.

That had worried him, and so he stopped.

The Wal-Mart parking lot was mostly empty by the time he got there, a row of cars by the only open door, a couple of RVs parked overnight, and not much else. He parked his truck in the back and killed the ignition. He was a few minutes early, but he didn't have to wait long for BH to show up. A small red Mazda parked alongside him. A short chubby dude got out of the car and climbed in next to Leo.

"Hey," said Black Hat, extending his hand for a handshake. It hung in the air awkwardly for a moment before Leo reached out and shook it, taking in the appearance of a man he only knew through text.

He was so *young*. Dressed in jeans and a hoodie too big for him, he wore glasses and had dark hair. He had no facial hair. Leo wouldn't put him past twenty-five. He could have been Leo's son.

"Trevor," said Black Hat. "My real name is Trevor."

"Right," said Leo. "Trevor. What info do you have?"

Trevor broke eye contact. He looked down on his hands.

He was nervous, struggling to collect himself. Leo could see that much.

"So, I realize I've only hinted at stuff before, about my life, but you should probably know more, just so you understand that everything is legit," said Trevor.

"Ok," said Leo. Trevor was talking fast, trying to get out a lot of information as quickly as he could.

"So, I work as a cyber-security consultant in the area, for a government contractor. I know it sounds vague as a job description, but it just means I handle IT and computer security for a bunch of different state agencies, and help build offerings for whenever they take on new contracts."

"Ok, computers," said Leo. "Did you hack something you weren't supposed to?"

"No," said Trevor. "Yes. Not really. It's complicated. I'm sorry. I'm still frazzled by this, and meeting you, and this late night secret rendezvous stuff—"

"Calm down," said Leo. "Finish your story."

"So we got a contract to dispose of a bunch of old equipment from congressional offices, that had been kept in storage for years and years. Old, old computers. Usually, on these types of jobs, I'm supposed to rip out the parts, erase the hard drives, and shred anything that could retain any trace of information. And I do—except I generally look at what's on the computers before I do that."

"That's where you've gotten the info you've given to me," said Leo.

"Yes," said Trevor. "Normally. I'm smart about it. If I felt they could trace it back to me, I don't give it to you. There's been some juicy stuff I've seen that I know would get me fired, so I let it go. But in the grand scheme of things, it's nothing, really. Receipts of senators using government money on vacations, proof of a judge's mistress, it's something, but never someone super important, and definitely would lead back to me."

He paused, and Leo was getting impatient, and more importantly, just plain tired. Was this a wild goose chase?

"And?" asked Leo.

"Sorry," said Trevor. "Well, we got all these old computers in, haven't been used in twenty years or so, been sitting in some warehouse or storage room or something. Dozens of them. So I'm going through them, and it's the usual nothing. Memos, speeches, spreadsheets, boring stuff. Then I come across a picture, taken with a digital camera, an old one, on a hard drive, buried under sub-folders. I don't know why it was there, but it's a big fucking deal."

Trevor dug into his pocket, and pulled out a folded up printout on white paper, and handed it to Leo. Leo looked around, but they sat alone in the parking lot. There was a distant roar of some engine, and then it receded.

He flipped on the overhead light and stared at the picture. It was a little pixelated, probably because of the quality of the camera used to take it. It was a picture of a bedroom. A crowd of unidentifiable silhouettes surrounded the bed. On the bed was a blond woman. A black man was on top of her, fucking her.

And that was it. Jesus, this was a wild goose chase. This kid dragged him out here because he found some swingers' pictures on some old computer.

"What the fuck is this, Trevor?" asked Leo. "I can get old pictures of black dudes screwing white chicks online without your help."

"I know, I know," said Trevor. "But this is different. I find a bunch of porn on these computers, but it's typically not like this. This was taken with a digital camera, a state of the art one at the time."

"Ok?" asked Leo. Trevor was driving at something, but Leo didn't know what.

"The camera. It gives us a time frame on the picture. Look at the woman. Look at her face."

Leo had only glanced at her before. He studied her now. She was older than at first glance, the far end of middle age, maybe even older, meaning her hair was dyed. The man mostly covered her body, but he could see her wedding ring on the hand that was showing. A married, older, blond woman. She looked familiar, but Leo was never great with faces.

"You don't recognize her?" asked Trevor. For the first time, Leo could sense admonishment in the kid's voice, like he had let him down.

"Kid," said Leo. "I was up at four AM, I worked all day, I don't have the energy for this."

Trevor glanced at him now, meeting his eyes again.

"That woman is Barbara Collins," said the kid, and everything shifted.

Barbara Collins had been the wife of Charlie Collins, a congressman that served for nearly forty years. He had been well respected. He had never lost an election and had been a constant in the Republican party for his entire tenure. The only reason he wasn't still serving was that he was dead, from a stroke at eighty-seven. Barbara was almost as famous, the archetypal politician's spouse. She had worked as a hostess for parties throughout Washington. Leo attended several, though none of them featured her getting plowed in front of the guests.

"Jesus," said Leo. He studied the picture. People surrounded the two of them, at least a dozen visible.

"That's not everything," said Trevor. "Look closer. Look at the figures in the back. You can make out a face."

Leo peered at it, the poor image quality not helping. He spotted the two men whose faces showed. The first, as hard as he tried, he couldn't identify. A generic looking dude in a button down.

"Holy shit," said Leo, as he looked at the other. He wasn't great with faces, but anyone who watched the news would recognize the other face, even if it was significantly younger. He was smiling in the picture, and the smile made it undeniable. It was him. It was Adam Simonson, the man who took over Charlie's seat, the man who was the current Speaker of the House, a potential future President. Wasn't a big leap who Warren's word from above came from.

"What the fuck was going on?" asked Leo. "Orgies with the Collins, with dozens watching, including Adam Simonson? Random black dudes fucking Barbara in front of everyone? This is crazy. The ratings will be fucking huge!"

Trevor sighed then, again, with disappointment. What was it now? What the hell was he missing?

"There's still more, Leo," said Trevor. "Look at the black guy, and think."

Leo looked at him, again at the picture. There wasn't much to see. He was slender, with close-cut hair. His face was mostly hidden, only the back quarter perspective of his head visible. He looked young. What else was he supposed to understand?

Trevor stared at him, waiting, waiting for Leo to recognize it.

"Give me a hint, something," said Leo, finally. This thing was a bombshell, but he couldn't push his mind any further.

"The Collins," said Trevor. "What were they known for? What charities did they represent? Think of their photo ops, back in the day. I know you've seen them."

Leo racked his brain. Charities? Photo ops? He thought back to the parties he went to, at their gigantic house, in the gated community. What stood out? Who was there?

And then he realized, and he understood why Trevor said that this would ruin lives.

Charlie Collins had always garnered so much bipartisan respect because he had seemed like a decent man, a good man. Starting in his fifties, Charlie pushed for a lot of international aid. He was an outlier in his party. Particularly in Africa, with the AIDS crisis and political instability. Charlie Collins put out calls to help African orphans, children who through no fault of their own faced unimaginable hardship.

Charlie had backed up his words with action. Thinking back to those parties, Leo remembered meeting a handful of African kids in that sea of white faces. A range of ages, all adopted by Charlie and Barbara Collins.

"I don't believe it," said Leo.

"I looked," said Trevor. "And I know we don't get a good view from the picture, but it wasn't hard narrowing it down, knowing roughly when it was taken, and looking up when they were adopted. It's the truth, right in front of us."

Trevor pointed at the photo, his finger aimed at the face of the black teenager on top of Barbara Collins, her face in ecstasy.

"That's Frederic Collins," said Trevor. "Their adopted son."

3

The arc was back in Leo's gut, all his frustration and lethargy gone. He was young again, a journalist and newsman again.

"I need everything," said Leo. "Everything you've got."

"There's not much else," said Trevor. He pulled out a thumb drive and handed it over to Leo.

"That's the entire computer I found it on. I captured an image of the whole thing and copied it everywhere. Nowhere online, though. Not safe."

Leo took the USB stick, in the palm of his hand.

"All of it fits on here?" asked Leo.

"It's an old computer," said Trevor.

"Where's the original?" asked Leo.

"Destroyed," said Trevor, after a pause. "I had to."

"What?" asked Leo. "You destroyed it? That's proof! We

need it."

"My time was up!" said Trevor, his voice finally raising. "I didn't know what to do, and I didn't want to get fired, but this is the biggest thing I've ever seen, a bunch of politicians fucking African kids for sport. If I get caught, that's it, that's my career. Companies like mine take this shit seriously. If they even knew I was looking at what was inside…"

He trailed off, and Leo saw him for what he was. A smart kid, who had attached himself to Leo, to his show, to his personality. Trevor was in over his head, but this wasn't Leo's first nervous informant.

"Calm down. Breathe," said Leo.

Trevor looked at him and took a breath.

"Is there anything else?" asked Leo. "Anything else you found on those computers? Even the slightest bit useful, more pictures, emails, hell, receipts for fucking cookies they served at their orgies."

"No, nothing," said Trevor. "I looked, scoured all of them. Nothing. I have no idea how that somehow still survived."

Leo had his theories. Charlie was an old man and didn't understand the danger of those things existing or of them spreading. The world wasn't as connected then.

"And this was Charlie's computer?" asked Leo.

"Hard to say," said Trevor. "They scrub most personal information before we ever get them. I'm ninety-five percent certain it was, but there's no direct proof."

"And there's nothing else," said Leo, not really a question anymore.

"No," said Trevor.

Leo held the photo in his hands, looking at it again. There was a world within that picture, hidden for two decades, and all he needed to do was shine a light on it. He would dig. He'd find out the truth behind it all, because of all his theories, the only one he believed without a shadow of a doubt was that this was only the tip of the iceberg. There was more here, and Leo would uncover it.

"How long have you sat on this?" asked Leo.

"A few months," said Trevor. "It felt like too much, you know? And we hadn't really been texting anymore, and so I was nervous about that. And then—"

"That's on me," said Leo, interrupting. "I'm not always an easy person to be friends with."

Trevor actually smiled at that. "Hey, man," said Trevor. "No worries. We're in this together now."

Leo said nothing, but Trevor was right. They were the only ones outside of that room who knew about this. He thought back to Warren's warning. How did they know something was coming if Trevor had sat on it for months?

"Have you talked to anyone else?" asked Leo. "Mentioned this at all?"

Trevor averted his eyes now. *Christ.*

"I, maybe, had discussed it on a dark web forum," said Trevor. "I know, it was dumb, but I was nervous, and I needed to talk to someone, and I was using an anonymous handle, and a VPN, and used only vague terms."

Enough for somebody, somewhere, to put something together. Leo only sighed.

"I'll be okay, right?" asked Trevor.

"Yeah, I think you'll be fine," said Leo. The fact that no one had tried to buy him out or silence him probably meant he was all right. And nobody knew about their connection.

"I can't get fired," said Trevor. "I need my job. I can't live with my parents again. My dad would kill me…"

"I'll protect you. You're an anonymous source. I'll dig into this, and I will break this thing wide open."

"Awesome," said Trevor. "Maybe I'll be able to sleep again."

"Been weighing on you?" asked Leo.

"I guess so," said Trevor. "Like, I've seen a lot of things in my job I've had to keep quiet, you know, and at first, I thought this would just be like that. Another thing I shouldn't know, and should probably just forget. But then I started having these dreams. Nightmares, really. Of something chasing me, and I would run and run, but I could feel it, I could feel its breath on the back of my neck, could feel it bite at my ankles."

"Did it catch you?" asked Leo.

"No," said Trevor. "It never did. But that was somehow worse. Because I wouldn't wake up then. I'd run away, and eventually, I'd get away. But the thing had a voice. And I'd get away, but the voice was with me, no matter how far I ran. And it screamed and screamed. So much rage in its voice."

"What did it scream?"

"Nothing," said Trevor. "It screamed nothing."

Trevor's voice was scary, and Leo wasn't sure if he wanted to know any more about Trevor's crisis of conscience. "Well, at least you can get that monkey off your back."

"Yeah, I hope so," said Trevor, and Leo felt like there was still something Trevor wasn't telling him. But he had enough for the night. The evidence was here. He just needed to do the work.

"I have to go," said Leo. "I've got to get up early tomorrow, and I'll be wiped already. I'll keep in touch, and make sure you're updated."

"Alright," said Trevor.

"Thanks for your help," said Leo.

"No problem," said Trevor, climbing down from the truck, and then he said something, but Leo didn't hear it, the summer breeze carrying it away.

"What'd you say?" asked Leo, Trevor closing the door, Leo asking through the window.

"I was going to tell you, earlier," said Trevor. "I was getting worried. I started hearing the voice."

"Which? The one from your nightmare?" asked Leo.

"Yeah," said Trevor, looking Leo in the eyes now. "I was hearing it when I was awake."

.

Leo looked into the camera, his gaze practiced, confident.

"The American flag is more than cloth, and it is more than just a representation of our family. It is a symbol, but one that stands for more than just America, not to say that's not important."

"Because it is, as important as anything. But it's important because of the sacrifices we've made over the years, the sacrifices our soldiers have made, our fathers, our grandfathers. Not just the soldiers, but the people who supported them. There's an entire network of people, all of whom paid a price to support this nation, support that flag. All paid some, some paid all."

"And that's what the flag really is, not a mere symbol of our country, but a symbol of the hard work, the effort, the blood paid to keep our country free, to keep it ours, to keep it safe and secure and the best damn country in the world, for years and years and years!"

Leo's eyes burned as he looked into the camera. *Do the work.*

"So when someone disrespects the flag, or our anthem, or our troops, that's why I get angry. That's why I can even get mean. Because it isn't just some flag they're disrespecting, not even the country they're disrespecting. They're disrespecting a legion of men and women who worked their fingers to the bone, who broke their backs, who pushed their own will to the limit, who died, for that flag, for this country. And I won't tolerate it."

The fire in his eyes faded. He looked at the other camera.

"That's our show for today. Thanks for watching, and remember, this is The Truth!"

Credits roll, and Leo looks through his notes until he hears "cut".

He gets the usual pats on the back and good jobs but he's not hearing any of it. All he can think of is that picture, and he hadn't had a moment alone with Warren to discuss it. It was folded up in his pocket. Leo had felt its weight all morning, a dumbbell dragging him down. He kept touching it, making sure it was there. It was precious. If he lost it, the story was gone.

Leo didn't stop for small talk after the show, beelining to his office. He needed to speak to Warren. Everything else was a distraction. He could hear John behind him, trying to flag him down.

"Leo, I was wondering if we could chat privately for a moment," said John, jogging to keep up with him.

"Sorry John, not today. Urgent business with Warren," said Leo, not even looking back. Whatever puff piece he wanted to run could wait for tomorrow's production meeting. He didn't see John's scowl.

He was almost running by the time he reached his office, shutting the door behind him, thudding as it shut. He didn't pour himself a drink. He needed to be sharp for this. Warren had warned him away from whatever it was, but that was before he knew. No one could deny the impact of this story. This could change the show and people's perception of him.

It felt like an eternity before Warren showed up, rapping on the door three times before entering, staring at his clipboard like usual.

"Good show, Leo," said Warren. "Great delivery on the flag stuff. People will eat that up. It'll be all over Twitter, I'm sure. I've already told the social media intern to spread it after it goes live. No drink?"

"Not today," said Leo. "Warren, your notes are important, but we need to talk about something bigger."

Warren looked up at him now, over his glasses. "Something bigger?"

Leo got up, pacing, his hand in his pocket, pulling out the picture, folded up, handing it to Warren.

"I had a meeting last night with an informant, and they showed me that," said Leo. "This is big, Warren. Bigger than any story I've ever broken in my entire life. We have to go after it." Leo was manic, the words just tumbling out of him. He was excited, a foreign feeling in this office lately.

Warren unfolded the printout and looked at it, his eyes scanning over it. His gaze moved back to Leo.

"What is this, Leo?" asked Warren, his voice low and collected. Warren always stayed calm, even with all the turmoil and chaos that passed through daily television news.

"It's a picture of Barbara Collins getting fucked by her own goddamn adopted son in a crowd full of socialites and politicians," said Leo, almost unable to contain himself. He was trying to keep his voice low, even if he had no real concern of anyone outside his office hearing them.

Warren looked back down at the picture and sighed. He folded it into its original shape and handed it to Leo.

"What are you doing, Leo?" asked Warren finally, looking at him now head on.

"I'm working, Warren," said Leo. "I'm doing what I should as the host and co-producer of the show, I'm finding stories that will get us ratings."

"What did I say yesterday, before you left?" asked Warren. Leo only looked at him. He hated this. Warren was treating him like his son. And he knew Warren would die before he broke. Leo gave him the answer he wanted.

"You said something big was coming down the pike, and to ignore it if I found it," said Leo.

"And you didn't listen," said Warren.

"This isn't some stupid report about a senator sending dick pics, Warren," said Leo. "This is huge. This involves dozens of people, adopted children forced to have sex, with some of the biggest politicians from the past twenty years. It is the very definition of a crazy conspiracy, that this time, just so happens to be totally fucking true. There could not be a story that is more appropriate for our show. The ratings will be through the roof, and earn us some goddamn credibility, which we so sorely need at the moment."

Warren didn't say anything. Leo was huffing and puffing, worked up. Finally, Warren spoke.

"Doesn't matter," said Warren, as if that was enough, the conversation ended.

"What do you mean, doesn't matter?" asked Leo. "It absolutely matters. Context fucking matters."

Warren took off his glasses and rubbed his eyes before replacing them.

"I shield you from our contacts up top," said Warren. "I keep you isolated. I do it because I think you work better when you're not handling that. And it has born out to be true. The show is consistently great, and a large part of that is you. But there's something I thought you understood, and just in case you don't, I will spell it out for you."

Leo wanted to interrupt, to scream, but he let Warren finish.

"Those men up top, who I shield you from, hold the show's fate in their hands. One phone call, and we're gone, you're gone, the show's gone. They control the decision makers, and we are small potatoes. Pawns. My advice to you is to forget that picture exists. To throw it away, to burn it, to destroy every copy of it, to tell your informant that you won't be investigating it. We are not investigative journalists. We are entertainers. If we follow that lead, John out there will have your job in a week, and I'll be most likely fired with you."

Warren's voice stayed composed and consistent the whole time, speaking to Leo in an even tone. It was driving Leo crazy. How the fuck could he be so calm about this?

"We have final editorial control," said Leo. "It's in my contract, Warren."

"Doesn't matter, Leo," said Warren. "We run after that, John will be sitting in your chair on Monday. I'll be lucky to keep my job. Some young gun would do it ninety percent as well for half as much. Drop it."

"Just forget the hottest story I've ever seen? This is Watergate, Warren," said Leo.

"I understand," said Warren. "But I don't want to hear any more. I don't want to be any more complicit. And as your executive producer, don't involve any more people here in this. It will only hurt them. It would be cutting our own throat."

Leo circled back around behind his desk, seeking shelter. He poured himself a drink and downed it in one gulp.

"But it's the truth, Warren," said Leo. "This isn't some made up bullshit conspiracy. This is the God's honest truth, and we're turning our backs on it." He stared at Warren, and Warren stared back at him. Warren looked at him not with anger or frustration, but with sadness.

"I thought you understood, Leo," said Warren. "Our audience doesn't want the truth, so we don't give it to them."

4

The circulating fan buzzed as Leo nursed his scotch. It was still hot as hell in his house, and he could feel the sweat running down his back.

He hadn't watched the show tonight. Goddamn piece of shit Warren. Always so fucking calm, telling him, *him,* Leo Price, host of the goddamned thing, what he could and couldn't run a a report on. Story of the year, maybe even story of the decade, and they just ignored it, let it lie.

Leo had done nothing. Warren had given him his notes for the day and then laid out the production meeting for tomorrow, and then left. Leo hadn't said a word, sat there like a glum fucking child and took it. If Warren cared, he hadn't shown it.

All the excitement, all the thrill of digging up the mystery was gone, dead. He sipped on the scotch, burning its way down his throat.

Warren was right. He *wasn't* a journalist. He was an entertainer, a host. He had said as much to John. He watched it every night, had seen every episode of The Truth, and it wasn't journalism. He was a fucking idiot for thinking otherwise for even a second.

He had heard the whispers back then. *Sell out. Shill. Hack.* Every party he went to had been filled with his friends and colleagues, the old-timers and the young idealists. He felt their eyes on him. They smiled politely, but under the surface they cursed him. Because he was leaving. Abandoning their profession.

Leo had fled a sinking ship. They had hated him because he didn't have the common decency to die with them. They all did the same in the end. McMichael went to TV. Angela Hill moved full time to sports writing. Diana wrote books. After all she said. After all the grandstanding and the platitudes, she had done the same thing he did.

He had known she felt that way. Leo had seen it in her eyes when she didn't think he was looking. He'd be working at his desk, and she'd glance at him, that same look of resentment, confusion, pity on her face.

The picture still weighed heavy in his pocket. He would have to tell Trevor that he wasn't pursuing the story. The cost was just too much. Leo couldn't afford to pay it. His career hung in the balance. He'd tell him to forget about the photograph and to stop digging around in computers that weren't his.

He stared at his phone and downed the rest of his glass. He texted Trevor.

Update on your lead: Have tried to pursue it, but have met with stiff resistance and threats to my career. I cannot continue. Would suggest you forget about it and move on.

Leo hit send and poured himself another drink. Sweat covered him, but he didn't care. The scotch was doing its work.

He waited for a reply. It didn't come. Trevor always replied quickly, and his silence felt like a judgment. He remembered the tone of Trevor's voice from the night before, the disappointment.

Leo picked up the phone.

I know you went through a lot of anguish about the decision to talk to me, but ultimately it is too costly to pursue. Hope you understand.

He sent it, his glass empty again. He refilled it, no ice.

No answer.

I sounded excited about it last night, but I got caught up in the story's potential. I'm not the right person to handle it. I could ask discretely through my contacts for someone who could do it correctly.

Could he pass it off, and get some shine from it without endangering his job? Diana would chase it. She'd see the value in it, with nothing holding her back from pursuing it. Hell, she could turn it into a book after. It wasn't in Trevor's hands anymore. It was in *his*.

Still no response.

Kid, I understand you're disappointed, but this is just the way things are sometimes. Keep your head down and I'll find something to do with the story.

Still no response, and then the phone buzzed in his hand, a call from Trevor. Leo answered.

"Kid, I'm sorry, but there's nothing I can do. My hands

are tied. Even a man in my position has to answer to certain people," said Leo, before Trevor could say anything.

"I'm glad to hear that," said a voice. Not Trevor's.

"Who the hell is this?" asked Leo.

"A friend," said the voice. Leo couldn't place it. It was male, low, but with little discernible accent.

"Where's Trevor, friend?" asked Leo.

"He's busy."

"What the fuck is going on?" asked Leo.

"It's probably best if you don't ask any more questions," said the voice, everything in his voice an implied threat.

"I don't fucking care—" said Leo, but the voice cut him off.

"Hey hey hey, one second there, Mr. Price," said the voice. "You know, not everyone gets a phone call. Like Trevor here. He didn't get one. But you, you get one, because of who you are. A courtesy call, so to speak."

They had found him. They had found Trevor.

"You've got a picture in your possession," said the voice. "You've shown it to your producer. You may or may not have copied it. Either way, here's the courtesy. Get rid of it, and forget it. Forget you've seen it. Forget you knew Trevor, or Black Hat, or whatever stupid alias he used."

"I—" started Leo, but the voice cut him off again.

"Tct," said the voice. "Not done yet."

"You do good work," said the voice. "I watch every night. Not my favorite, but the boss tells me it's important. You spread the good word, so to speak. That's me editorializing, but I hope you especially can forgive me for that. We don't want that."

"You fucker, where's Trevor?" asked Leo.

"So angry," said the voice. "We don't want to pull you off your show. We want you to keep up your good work. Missed tonight's show, been busy, but yesterday's was great. Loved that lemonade stand bit. So that's all this is. A warning. Keep it to yourself, and this will all be a bad dream."

"Who's paying you?" asked Leo. "Simonson? Who?"

"That would be telling," said the voice. "And it doesn't really matter. Let it go, Mr. Price. You're past the point of investigating real stories anyhow."

Leo began to yell and then it went dead. Leo called Trevor again, and Trevor's voicemail answered, Trevor's young voice promising that he'll get back to him.

Leo squeezed the phone, the screen twisting before he let go. Some fixer got to Trevor. God knows where he was or if he was alive.

He had no more information on him. He had his email, a phone number. No address, no assurances that Trevor was even his real name, and now he was missing.

What the hell could he do?

He should have known. He should have realized the risks. He promised Trevor he would protect him, and he spouted his mouth off to Warren at the first opportunity. Did he think it would be easy? Just free and clear, ruin the lives of dozens of people? His job was where it *started*.

He poured himself another drink, and then more after that.

Leo could see the man's face, as the fixer dragged Trevor through the swamp. He didn't hide it. There was no one there besides the two of them, the man and Trevor. The man had a thick mustache, black eyes, and a simple haircut, with close-shorn black hair. He seemed to be in his mid-forties, but it was dark.

Leo saw his eyes, as he took Trevor to a deep, wet place where no one would ever see him again.

His eyes looked bored.

Leo followed them. He had no choice.

It was dim, but Leo could see the swamp, the muck and mire that this fledgling country was built upon. The water was shallow here. The man led Trevor like he knew the way, his flashlight shining a cone of light on mud and cypress trees. Trevor was wearing sweatpants and a t-shirt, his tennis shoes soaked and covered in sludge. Small noises came from him. The man ignored the sobs and moans, marching Trevor deeper into the marshland. They walked for a long time.

There was a cabin, then. No, not a cabin, a shack, a wooden shack, that was only ten by ten feet. Ugly but sturdy. It didn't have to be more than that, because the only ones who saw it were the man and the people he brought out here to question and then kill. Trevor was the latest one.

He dragged Trevor into the shack, and Leo followed them.

There wasn't much inside. A battery-powered lamp hung from the ceiling, and the man turned it on, white light filling the small space. A chair sat underneath it, metal and thick. There was a duffel bag in the corner.

He dumped Trevor in the chair, and Trevor didn't struggle. The man duct taped Trevor's arms and legs to it, and then ripped off the black hood covering his head. The fight in him was gone. Leo saw why. It had been beaten out of him, his face a black and bloody mess, his nose broken, his eyes swollen. Duct tape covered his mouth, and the man ripped it off. Trevor yelled in pain. His split lip started bleeding again. The man had battered him and dragged him into the swamp.

Trevor's head hung down. He didn't have the strength to hold it up.

"Don't worry, Trev," said the man. "This will all be over soon. Just a few more questions and then we'll be done."

The man pulled out pliers and bolt cutters from the bag in the corner. Leo wanted to give up now. Trevor wasn't leaving this room alive, and the terror rising in Leo's chest was something he couldn't bear any more. He urged himself to leave, to run away, but he was unable. Leo was stuck in place. His eyes remained open. He would watch and see the cost that Trevor would pay for spreading the truth. Leo was forced to watch.

"Who did you tell?" asked the man.

"I told you," said Trevor, without looking up. "I told Leo, and that's it."

"Just checking," said the man. "Sometimes people change their story, and there's nothing that frustrates me more. Telling the truth is all you have to do. Just a couple more questions."

He grabbed the bolt cutters, and opened them, placing Trevor's right pinky finger in between the blades. He left it there. Leo looked at it, the small piece of flesh exposed to danger. A minimal amount of pressure and Trevor is short one digit.

"P-please—" said Trevor, whimpering.

"Shhh, shh, shhh," said the man. "Answer my questions truthfully, and you'll keep your fingers. Did you find any other files besides that picture?"

"No," said Trevor. Leo's eyes remained glued to the bolt cutter. It stayed where it was.

"Just one more question," said the man. "Where's all the physical evidence?"

"My PC and laptop," said Trevor. "I destroyed the original hard drive. Shredded it."

Trevor screamed as the man squeezed the handles of the big tool and cut off Trevor's pinky finger, blood pouring out. Leo couldn't look away.

"So close," said the man. "I know Leo has a copy. But you were close. You did well."

Trevor was sobbing now, tears and blood mixing on his broken face. He was trying to say something, but it came out as unintelligible babble.

The man dropped the bolt cutters and pliers back into the pack in the corner, grabbing rope instead.

"What was that, Trev?" asked the man, his movement relaxed.

Trevor caught his breath. "Leo will expose you. He'll expose this whole thing."

The man tied the heavy cord into a familiar knot, his hands practiced.

"Is that right?" asked the man, not looking at Trevor.

"You and your bosses will have your faces plastered all over the fucking news," said Trevor. He spat out blood.

The man finished his work with the rope, and then pulled out a phone from his pocket. Trevor's phone. He turned it on. He read from it. Leo recognized the words. It was his text messages from earlier in the night.

The fixer read them.

"Update on your lead: Have tried to pursue it, but have met with stiff resistance, and threats to my career. I cannot continue. Would suggest you forget about it and move on."

"I know you went through a lot of anguish about the decision to come to me, but ultimately it is too costly to pursue. Hope you understand."

The man read them and then showed them to Trevor's face. His eyes, behind bruised and swollen eyelids, scanned them, and then he cried, blood hanging from his mouth as his body was wracked with sobs.

YOU PROMISED TO PROTECT HIM

Leo winced. Pain washed through him, through whatever form he inhabited here. He tried to breathe, but he couldn't.

The man held the rope out in his hands, and Leo saw it for what it was. A noose. He slid the loop over Trevor's neck as he cried. Trevor didn't struggle. He had given up. The man cinched it tight and then cut the tape binding Trevor to the chair. He pulled Trevor out of the chair, and pulled him out the door. Trevor stumbled after him, grabbing at the leash with his nine fingers.

"Please don't," said Trevor, mumbling at the man. "Please, don't. Please, my wife, she—"

The man tugged and Trevor fell. His strength was gone. The man circled back around behind Trevor. The noose was tight. All the man did was pull.

The rope cut into Trevor's neck. He tried to slide his fingers in between as his brain shut down. His mouth foamed and he grunted as the man strangled him, his knees wet in the muddy swamp. The frogs chirped in the distance as Trevor died. The man held the noose taut for two full minutes, long after Trevor stopped struggling.

Leo saw none of this.

As soon as Trevor fell, Leo saw the woman, standing at the edge of darkness, staring at him. Not at Trevor. At *Leo.* Trevor died and she screamed. Leo heard everything she knew.

5

Leo could feel every ounce of ache in his body while he stared at the camera. He was sweating through his makeup, and his stammering had ruined multiple takes already.

She was there. The woman in the darkness, the one who screamed. She had crept in at the edge of his vision and she would not stop.

He had woken up that morning in a pile of vomit, his pants wet from pissing himself. He found two empty bottles of scotch in the sink.

It wasn't a dream, or a nightmare. He had seen Trevor die, had watched the fixer who talked to him kill the kid after beating and torturing him. Out in the fucking swamp somewhere. Frozen, forced to watch. The alcohol hadn't done that. It was *her*.

And the booze hadn't made her appear. The wraith that lurked in the shadows of Trevor's death, a silhouette at the edge of shadow. It grew fuzzier every minute. He couldn't picture the fixer's face anymore. The shack and the conversation between the two men had all but vanished.

The woman wouldn't fade. She stared at him with her wide, unblinking eyes, bent into anger and outrage and fury. He knew she was there. All he could see were her eyes, glowing at him out of the darkness of the swamp.

They followed him. He was reading the teleprompter and he could swear that she was there. She lurked right beyond the camera. Her damnable eyes stared and accused him.

And he was acting like a fucking amateur, missing cues and sweating like a pig. His goddamn hands were shaking, for fuck's sake, being a child, being some pussy that couldn't handle the pressure. *You're Leo Price.* Act like it.

Her eyes are there

John's segment played, a piece about firemen in Alaska losing their firehouse dog but then raising all of her puppies in her stead. It was heart-touching, as always, but Leo couldn't watch it. He could barely stay awake.

He didn't get back to sleep last night. He had woken up at three thirty in the morning in his own filth. He had cleaned himself, changed, and downed nearly a gallon of water with twice the recommended dosage of Tylenol. All Leo wanted was to disappear for a few hours of sleep, but she waited for him when he closed his eyes. It wasn't dark behind them anymore. *She* was there now.

His head was pounding. He needed silence and rest. If you make it through the day, you can go home. Figure out what to do about Trevor, about the phone call, about the story, about that woman.

It was time for his closing monologue. *Focus, Leo.*

"Thank you for that, John," said Leo, turning to face the other camera.

"Every day, there's a new study, a revelation that disproves an old one, about our bodies, about our health. I try and keep up with it, but it seems more and more a fool's errand. I say this because every day there are more and more people trying to criticize people's decisions about their well-being. About what doctors they see, about what medicine they take—"

Her scream interrupted him, stopped him in his tracks, shut him down. He winced, the pain gripping him like a kick in the balls. It drove the air out of him. He dug his fingers into his palms. His lungs froze as he tried to catch his breath, unable to talk or think. He felt it all again. The overwhelming horror from last night washed over him, all at once.

"You ok, Leo?" asked Warren's voice, from the control room. Leo glanced around, frantic, his eyes darting to the various crew standing behind the cameras. They were watching him. They hadn't heard it, hadn't *seen* it.

Breathe.

"Yeah," said Leo. "Sorry about that. I'll restart from the last line."

He breathed, blinked—*her eyes*—and looked into the camera again.

"About what doctors they see, about what medicine they take. And—and everyone's personal health, their decisions over their health, are only their own. We are so quick to judge if someone is unsure about vaccinations, or if they prefer medicines that aren't doled out by Big Pharmaceutical."

"I'm not saying you should distrust every doctor, but…"

Leo was faltering. He could feel the paper dampen in his hands.

"But medicine is still a complicated and personal issue, with no clear answers. Thanks for watching, and don't forget, this is The Truth!"

He waited for the cameras to turn off, staring at the papers on his desk. Warren yelled cut from the control room and Leo could breathe again. He was soaked through with sweat. Now he needed to get to his office, and then go the hell home, and—

"Rough night, Leo?" asked John, from behind him. "You doing all right?"

John could fuck off. Leo didn't have time for this shit. He beelined down the hallway, ignoring John.

Then a hand closed on his shoulder, and Leo swung around, his fist in the air. John winced, raising his hands, palms out, warding off Leo.

"Whoa, fella," said John. "I just wanted to talk. You keep putting it off."

Leo lowered his fist, now pointing at John, his finger right in his face.

"I know exactly what the fuck you're doing," said Leo, raising his voice. The crew turned toward the argument.

"No need to yell," said John, staying calm. Oh, this motherfucker. Leo's head was killing him. The woman's eyes shot at him from a shadow behind John, and Leo couldn't take it anymore. John wanted a confrontation; he was getting one.

"Don't you dare tell me what to fucking do," said Leo. "I

was building this show when you were still in high school, feeling up girls through their sweaters. No matter how many goddamn puff pieces about firemen and lemonade stands and puppies you do. You will never sit in my chair."

John's voice was low. He smiled, even as Leo's index finger was an inch from his face.

"You're losing your touch, old man," said John. "The world is changing, and the show will change too. You're a dinosaur."

"I've always been ahead of the game, you piece of shit," said Leo. "This isn't any different. There's always someone like you, who can't do anything on your own, who has to climb on top of somebody else to get anywhere." Leo wasn't being quiet, and everyone heard what he said. The studio was silent.

"We have a problem here?" asked Warren, storming in from the control booth. He stopped next to the two men, Leo's finger still in John's face.

"No problem at all, Warren," said John, backing away. "I was just wishing Leo well. He was struggling out there today. Happens to the best of us." John left.

Leo stood there, sweating, shaking with rage.

"Leo," said Warren, quietly.

Leo didn't answer. Her eyes lingered there, he knew it, someone strangled Trevor, it was his fault, he couldn't—

"Leo," said Warren. "You look like shit. Let's go to your office." He touched Leo. Leo saw what he looked like in reflected in Warren's face. They turned and walked to his office.

The big door shut behind them.

"What the fuck are you doing?" asked Warren, his voice

calm.

"He knows what he's doing, Warren," said Leo. "John is doing this shit on purpose."

"Of course he is," said Warren. "But you can't jump at him. And you sure as hell can't scream at him, can't raise your hand to him in front of God and the whole crew. It's what he wants, and you're playing directly into his hands. I know you're smarter than this. You've dealt with this before. You're better than him. Stay that way and he'll leave, move to greener pastures."

He knew Warren was right. He had handled this before everywhere he'd worked. There was always someone young and hungry who wanted your spot. There was a limited number of them. If you had one, you had a target on your back.

He didn't care.

"Fire him," said Leo.

"He's too valuable," said Warren.

"Fuck him," said Leo. "Let him be too valuable somewhere else."

"The network wants him here," said Warren. "And it's not a hill I'm willing to die on." Warren's words chilled Leo. Trevor dying while that woman stared. Trevor chose his when he handed off the photo. He didn't know it, though.

"Which hill is that?" asked Leo, his head raging. *Let me go home, Warren.*

"Excuse me?"

"Which hill is the one you're willing to die on?" asked Leo.

Warren ignored the question. "You look like shit, Leo. And John was right. You were bad."

"I had a rough night," said Leo. "Drank too much."

"I don't care how much you drink," said Warren, "but the second you bring it on the air is the second that you start becoming a liability."

"It won't happen again," said Leo. The mere thought of alcohol was enough to make him puke.

He didn't know if he could sleep without it.

"One more day, and then we have the long weekend," said Warren. "Take it slow. Rely on your instincts. And for god's sakes, don't let John get under your skin. The network loves him, and don't make it easy on them by punching him in the face."

Leo hunched over his desk and looked at Warren. He wanted to reveal everything. Warren was the closest thing to a confidant he had. Leo yearned to tell him about Trevor and the vision. About that woman and her accursed eyes, following him.

But he said nothing. How had the fixer known he talked to Warren? The fixer didn't have goddamn magic powers, and Leo refused to believe they had bugged his office. Warren had reported to someone. And it had cost Trevor his life.

He wanted to heap the blood onto Warren's back, but he needed to carry it himself. They were all against him.

"I'm going home," said Leo.

He found the missing persons report quickly. Trevor Williams, twenty-two, filed at 4 PM yesterday.

Who filed it? Trevor didn't have much of an online identity. No social media and no marriage license. He scrubbed it pretty well or never engaged with it at all. The picture was him, though.

They'd never find the body. Even if Leo told them, they

still might not discover it. The swamp was thousands of square miles, uninhabited, and hard to cover. The fixer knew what he was doing.

Leo didn't doubt that what he witnessed in the vision was true. He didn't know why he was shown it, but he felt it's truth. Trevor was dead, rotting in some bog somewhere in the Maryland swampland.

With that same confidence, he knew whatever that creature was, was as real as Trevor's death. Her eyes and that scream told him. They had a permanence that was as real as the sun and moon.

He couldn't remember what she said. She didn't say anything, but she screamed, and it spoke for her. Her scream contained everything, and it hurt. It rattled him inside.

He had turned on all the lights, after he wiped up his puke and threw his pants in the wash, the night before. He had closed all the drapes and lit up every bulb in the house. It would keep her away, he had thought. He had left them on all day. The AC still wasn't working, and his home was stifling hot.

He wouldn't open the windows. He turned on the fans, and drank glass after glass of ice water, trying to rehydrate. He swallowed six ibuprofen, hoping they would dull the headache.

She had retreated since her outburst. Leo knew it. He felt her absence.

In the vision, as she screamed at him, Leo understood what she was. In that moment, he understood. Not now. It was all an ominous blur. It was gone in the haze, along with the fixer's identity, the location of the shack.

What could he do?

Go to the cops. Would they find anything, any evidence? Leo's information about a vague shack somewhere in a swamp would give them nothing.

Dig deeper. Turn up more evidence, investigate, and unearth everything about the Collins, the picture, and everyone involved. Punish them.

Give up. Forget it all happened. Go back to his normal life and his show. Worry about John taking his job and the typical stress.

The latter was retreat. Cowardice. But he wouldn't die, alone, strangled in a swamp. He wasn't invincible, and no one was safe.

His headache dulled. All he wanted now was to sleep. But could he risk turning the lights off? The shadows were her domain.

One light off. That's all he would need. He turned off his bedroom lamp, the dim glow from the hall and bathroom filtering into the room. Just enough darkness for him to get some sleep, which he craved at this point. Just a brief break.

The wood creaked on the first floor, beneath his room.

She had been gone, he was certain, and a part of him was sure it was because he had filled the house with brightness and closed the drapes. He had warded off the monster. He did what you do when you need to keep a horror out. She wouldn't leave the darkness.

He was a fool for doing it, and even more of one for believing it worked.

Whatever she was, the light would do nothing to stop her, and she was here.

6

Leo was tired. He was tired of this spirit and tired of this mystery. The anger, the frustration that John had tapped into earlier was there again. Leo didn't care what this thing was, this was *his* home, and he would have no more part of it.

He grabbed the Desert Eagle from his nightstand drawer, loaded it, and thumbed off the safety. It was heavy, the metal cold in the warmth. He was Leo Price, goddamnit.

He turned the lamp back on in his bedroom, and he swept the house. If that thing was here, he would kill her, drive her away. *He* controlled his life.

He started with his room, throwing open closet doors, shining a flashlight under the bed. Any nook or cranny, he would unearth her. Leo would force her out.

The master bath, bright white light bouncing off the tiles, the mirrors, the glass. Nothing.

The floor reverberated as Leo pounded down the upstairs hallways, his pistol tight in his hand. The two guest bedrooms were next. He dumped the mattresses on the hardwood, ripping open closet doors. It had no space for the ghastly woman thing, but he exposed it anyway. He pulled out the spare towels, sheets, comforters. There was no place in *his* house for her.

The floors creaked downstairs and Leo set after the noise. He eliminated all shadow. He tipped over the couch and chairs. Nowhere to hide. The closets were opened, boxes and plastic tubs were hauled out and upended. She was here somewhere. He felt her.

A sound. The den.

Leo marched there and pushed over the armchairs, covered in sweat now. It dripped off of him as he tore through the house. The summer heat had piled up all day. He pulled up rugs. She was underneath them; he knew it. That's where she hid. She didn't leave earlier. She was still here.

His study. His desk, heavy and beautiful. It weighed hundreds of pounds. He strained, the muscles in his legs and back quavering. Then it shifted, tipped, fell over, the house shaking as it landed. His computer, books, and papers all crashed to the floor. Replaceable. He would find her. He would drive her out.

The kitchen! It was a huge space, modern and bright. Leo opened the pantry, dumping boxes of cereal on the ground, oatmeal, any container that contained darkness, that's where she was, that's where she *was*. The fridge, the freezer. He flung the doors open, the cold air a small blessing that

Leo didn't stop to cherish.

The house was full of light. The furniture was toppled over, and empty of any spirit.

Wait.

The garage. That was where she was. The light. He had turned it off when he came inside, a force of habit. He flew in, turning it on. His pistol was up and ready.

There was nothing in there but his cars. He looked underneath, but they would have to remain bastions of shadow. He kept it clean, and there was nowhere else for her to hide.

He hurried back to the house, the manic burst of energy draining out of him. He needed sleep. She wasn't here. He was sure of it. But he knew what drew her to him. What it all started with.

The photograph. It was the source of all this trouble. Trevor had told him, had warned him. Trevor had heard the voice. Had the nightmares. It was the picture. It carried that scourge with it.

His sleep, his sanity, his job, his life. He was risking it all for that picture, for its story. It wasn't worth it. The truth came at too high a cost. As long as he possessed it, that wraith would haunt him.

He ran back to his computer, toppled on the floor. A single crack extended the length of his monitor, but it still turned on. He deleted his backups and copies.

The thumb drive. He grabbed it and rushed into the kitchen. He needed to destroy it. Leo dropped it down the garbage disposal, turned on the water, and flipped the switch. It whirred into action, and the awful cacophony told him the machine did its job.

Only the hard copy remained. The printout was still in his coat pocket.

He pulled it out and studied it again. Barbara and Frederic Collins. Her wedding ring. The face of Speaker Adam Simonson.

He should burn it. Destroy it. With nothing left, he would be safe again. No more phone calls, no more fixers, no more problems at work. He would reclaim his position from John and relegate him to the lemonade stands forever. He was a newsman, goddamnit.

He returned to his office, his breath coming short. So goddamn hot. Sweat was pouring off of him, but soon it would be over. He could lie down in the dark again. Get back to his normal life.

He found what he was looking for, his lighter. It was heavy, engraved with his initials. It had been a gift from his son Alex. Leo had smoked cigars, from time to time. Stopped by doctor's orders.

He thumbed the lighter, feeling the metal in his hand. He flicked, and a large bright yellow flame shot up, satisfying and hot. The light would destroy her, just like the photo. He was sure of it now.

The picture in his other hand. That was twenty years ago. Why revive it, Leo? To seek some notion of truth? He drew the paper closer to the fire. Sleep again. Peace, again.

His phone rang in his pocket, and he jumped, dropping the lighter. It clacked shut on the floor.

Goddamnit. He caught a glimpse of himself in his office mirror. Half naked, covered in sweat. He looked mad. The phone continued to ring. He answered.

"Hello?" he said.

"Hello," said a female voice that Leo didn't recognize. "Is this Leo Price?"

"Speaking," said Leo.

"Hi, Mr. Price," said the voice. "I'm Laura Williams."

Who? Leo didn't know any Laura Williams.

"I'm sorry, ma'am," he said. "I don't know you. I'm going to—"

"No, we've never met," said Laura. "But you know my husband."

"I don't know any Mr. Williams," he said. "I—"

"Trevor," said Laura. "Trevor Williams. He said you had struck up a friendship after he helped you with some stories for your show."

Trevor's wife. He *was* married. She must have filed the missing persons report.

"How did you get this number?" he asked.

"I—I found it in Trevor's things," she said. "I was gone on business, and when I came back, he was gone, just gone. This isn't like him at all. He's always so routine, always dependable."

"I'm sorry," said Leo. "I don't—"

"He had texted me," she said. "Two days ago. Told me he might have something for you again—that's why I called. Just wondering if he's contacted you, if you've seen him, or heard from him. I don't know what to do."

He's dead Laura, choked to death in a dark swamp, his only companions a cold-blooded murderer and a dead-eyed wraith. His body is sunk in a bog somewhere, rotting. They'll never find it. You'll never learn what actually happened to him. He disappeared one day, the man you love, and he's never coming back.

"I haven't talked to him recently," said Leo. "He last text-ed me six months ago, or so."

"Oh," said Laura. "It seemed like much more recent than that."

"Sorry," said Leo. "I have a lot of sources, but I wish you the best of luck in finding him. I need to go."

"Wait," she said. "Before you go. Thank you. For talking to him, for working with him. Trevor absolutely loved your show, watched it every night. He was lost for a while, after we moved here, but when he told me that he was messaging you, and giving you news stories—he became a new man. You brought him a lot of joy. So thanks."

"Bye," said Leo, and hung up.

He still held the picture in his other hand, his fingers gripped into a fist, crumpling it. The lighter lay at his feet. He could burn it, give himself this peace. Forget about Trevor. Trevor wasn't his fault. Trevor dug up something he shouldn't have, and it killed him. It will cost you everything. *Destroy it, Leo.*

No. He smoothed out the printout, folding it neatly. He went to the wall, flipping back a framed photo, the single place he didn't look for the woman, the spirit with the searing gaze. His safe. He keyed in the combination, opened the door, and placed the printout inside.

He wouldn't burn it. Not yet. No one would know the difference. The photograph was collateral. He wasn't a victim. Not Leo Price. It would be protected, and he would be out of danger. He'd leave Simonson and whoever else be. After his job was secure, Leo could go after the story. He could still break it. He was a newsman.

The place was a mess, and he was so tired. No sleep in

forty-eight hours. It seemed absurd now, all of it. A specter showing him Trevor's death, following him around? Hiding in his home? Too much booze, not enough sleep. After a good night's sleep, he could think everything through.

He walked through the house, his strength ebbing, cleaning up everything. He righted furniture, discarded food in the kitchen, turning off lights as he went. He piled things back in various closets, unworn clothes, knick-knacks, old Christmas gifts he never used. He would sort through them later.

Laura Williams's thank you kept entering his mind, and he pushed it aside. Leo opened the windows and the hot air bled out. The sweat dried on his body. He could breathe again.

The memories of the workday, the nightmares, and the visions of death were all fading away. He was too tired to hold on to them. The house was clean now, neat enough. The lights were out and a refreshing breeze swept through the space. He could sleep now.

He washed his face and retreated to his bed, turning off the last light. The mattress was soft and comforting. He would wake up fresh and start his life again, back to the normal grind. He would forget about Trevor and that picture. Leo would forget about *her.*

He drifted away.

SNAP

The noise brought him back. He woke up from the verge of sleep, listening for the sound. Something from outside? No.

He had just married Diana. They'd just moved into their home on the beach, their dream house. You could hear the waves crashing in. It had groaned and creaked, snapped and popped. He got used to it, eventually, but initially, the snaps would wake him. He would prowl through the dark, looking for intruders, for drunks stumbling in off the sand. He only had a baseball bat then. The gun came later, one of the first sticking points between him and Diana. She didn't want a weapon in their home.

He had never found anything. The old wooden building had constantly adjusted to the humidity, to the wind, to the ground. He slept through the clatter, eventually.

There's nothing there, Leo. That thing, that woman, isn't real. You're hallucinating. You need sleep. Fall asleep again.

He listened, and tried to sleep. But it didn't come. Everything ached, and his eyes begged for rest, but his mind explored the dark and the clamor.

Diana kept the beach house after the divorce. He could have fought her for it, but he gave her what she wanted. The split was bloodless. In truth, he had been glad to not sleep there anymore. He never liked the noise.

Before he bought this one, he made the seller let him sleep a night in it. It was on the market for a long time, so they agreed to the request. Leo brought in an air mattress and slept in the empty master bedroom. It was silent, and he put in the official offer the next day.

This house didn't make noise, and it wasn't from outside. *Go to sleep, Leo.*

He couldn't. He would turn on the light. He would see that it was empty, and he would sleep.

He got up, using his phone as a flashlight, his eyes wincing at the screen's brightness in his face. He walked to the switch and flipped it on.

His bedroom would be empty, and he would sleep.

Light filled the room, and she was there, right there.

And she screamed.

7

Her eyes. Piercing black that burned through whatever they saw. They had stared at him out of the darkness of the swamp, while someone killed Trevor. They had watched him from the edges of his vision.

It was all he remembered, all he imagined when he had torn through his house.

She was more than her gaze.

She was there, looming over him, nine, ten feet tall, her head scraping against the ceiling, taller than that, her body bent to fit in the room. Her skin was sallow, white, bloodless, stretched across a massive, lanky frame, elongated limbs and torso, her surface pulled back, her neck, fingers, long, longer. Her charcoal hair defied gravity, floated around her, a obsidian cloud that enveloped them both, a cowl that swirled and flowed, alive.

Her eyes. Starless orbs that dominated her face, lidless, they saw him and everything. Her nose was shrunken down to cartilage and bone, her mouth an open stygian maw rimmed with dozens of tiny, jagged teeth, as white as her skin.

Her arms outstretched, longer than she was tall, her alien fingers tipped with sharp bone, blackened, charred. She was naked, her breasts deflated, her body hairless. She had no fat, no muscle, only skin and bone, a blood-drained wraith.

Leo screamed.

When he was six, on vacation in Florida with his parents, exploring a park, he discovered an ant hill. Being a six-year-old, he dug, unearthing tunnel after tunnel, more and more ants filing out of the dirt. He didn't realize how many there were, and that they were covering him. They bit him. Thousands of ants chewing on him, their venom flowing into his tiny frame. He screamed and screamed. His parents found him, doused him in water. He spent the night in the emergency room, his body red and swollen, vomiting from the toxin.

Leo screamed like a child covered in ants, falling backward, away from her, anything to put some distance between them. But he wasn't heard.

Her scream was everything, and Leo was not heard by her or anyone else. It buffeted him, a force, sheer power hitting him like a jet engine, a hurricane. He scuttled away from her, but she leaned over him, her frame filling his vision, dark hair and dark eyes and alabaster skin. It hit him, driving into him, seeping into him, filling him up. Dense as a dead star, gravity pulled him into the floor. Her scream would kill him.

He felt it, the volume piling up inside, rising coldly from his toes. He shriveled as he filled.

She continued. The sound was encompassing, and she pushed closer and closer to him, her mouth open wide, a third black socket to match her eyes. Closer, closer, a foot away, now six inches. She would drown him.

He swung at her before it reached his arm, a feeble attempt to drive her off, his pistol behind him, in his nightstand, a dozen steps from him, a world away.

Leo swiped at her, and it only enraged her. He would swear he hit her, his fist connecting with her chin, but he felt no impact. Her massive hand wrapped around his throat and scooped him up without effort, his dense body off the ground, up, pressed hard against the ceiling above them both. She drove the air out of him, and he couldn't breathe.

She didn't stop screaming, her mouth below him, the tiny teeth stone white against the dark maw that filled him with dreadful sound. He could feel it, even as he struggled for breath. She was killing him, liquid noise in his chest, his neck, his head. Leo was dying.

He was full, and then he saw.

It was darkness, at first. Then the hood was ripped off, his arms and legs bound to the chair he sat in. It was bright, the single bulb hurting his eyes until they adjusted. He saw the man who captured and beat him.

The blood was running down his face, and he tried to spit it out, his jaw aching, teeth missing. He sobbed, crying, sputtering because he knew then he would die here. He understood if this man was letting him see him, he was never leaving this bog. The man talked to him. Hurt him. But there was nothing else for him.

All of this for the truth. The man had dragged him into the swamp like a sick dog, and he looked out into the darkness. He saw her. Her eyes were dark but he saw them, and they looked not at him, not at the man, but past them and he died, his knees wet in the mud. He thought of Laura.

The room was full of men, men of power. He stood by the wall, leaning against it, shoulder to shoulder with two other men he didn't recognize. He wore a suit, like many others here, although some loosened their ties, removed their coats, rolled up their sleeves.

The bedroom was crowded, the bed the only furniture, no chairs or dressers. It served a single purpose. It was his first time, a virgin they had called him at dinner. He didn't have the specifics, but this was his ticket to his future.

He would be President one day. He was young still, still crafting relationships, but Charlie tucked him under his wing and watched him. Staying there was key, whatever it cost. They respected Charlie, and he would ride that gravy train as far as it would travel.

The parties were a part of it, a whispered secret, a wink and a nod. Charlie invited him after a year under Charlie's wing. He accepted because he wasn't a fool. But this was only the beginning, only the start. Because the real invitation was to the room, with only a select few allowed to attend.

He was let into the room two years later. It was sacrosanct and his future rode on being there. So he watched and worked, and stayed under Charlie's wing. And he got his invitation.

And now he saw what happened in the room, which no one would say. Barbara Collins, naked on the bed, putting her mouth on that African kid they adopted. What the fuck. This is what he waited for?

But he stayed, and he watched, just like everyone else.

He saw the hallway. It was long. It stretched out in front of him, the carpet dark red, the wallpaper flowers and pixies and fairies, dancing in the garden. He walked down it and his stomach ached because he dreaded the end.

The doors were wooden, and heavy, on each side, soldiers lining up as he passed. Door after door, the hallway that never ended.

Except it did end, and he knew what was there. Leo knew what waited for him. There was no stopping it. This was home now, and there was nowhere to run.

His hand was small, subsumed by the fist that held it and pulled him down the corridor. It grabbed him tight and it would not let go. It was cold and clammy, and it held. He didn't resist, not anymore. It was worse when he did. That made it all worse, made the terror hurt more.

He stared up at the figure that held him. It dragged him and gripped his hand with a prescribed false tenderness. It glanced back down, a rictus grin smiling down on him, teeth showing, cheeks red. His eyes gleamed with excitement, his tongue crossing over his lips and gums. It was Charlie Collins, alive.

The infinite hallway ended in a door, one that matched the dozens of others they passed. It opened, and inside was pain, and shame, and horror.

Leo opened his eyes again, and she was still there. Her hand held him tight, her otherworldly strength pushing him hard against the ceiling. She screamed and her language of volume washed over him and vision after vision pushed through him, of abuse and rape. She was speaking to him, preaching to him, showing him the truth, an unknowable truth, a complete picture that no one possessed. But she did, and she taught it to him. He had no breath, and the truth filled and trapped him. He saw Charlie Collins, and his children, and every man that accepted the invitation, each and every degree of guilt, a spectrum of sin.

And then it ended, and she was gone, and he was on the floor, and he could breathe.

He gasped, air filling his lungs for the first time in years, years spent with her filling him with her gospel. She showed him everything. He knew her name like he knew his own.

Truth.

He sat up, his vision swimming as blood rushed to his head. The house was quiet, the slight wind rushing through the open windows, his skin dry. He stared at the clock. No time had passed.

She filled him with images, repeating over and over and over again. So many, arcing through his mind like lightning. The smile of Charlie Collins looking down at him, within easy reach.

The screams. Someone would have heard them. He peered outside, out onto the quiet street he lived on. Nothing. No wandering eyes, no questioning glares. A dog barked somewhere. No one had heard him, or her. Impossible. It was all impossible.

He needed to sleep, to rest. Leo would wake up early and get back to work. He would forget about it all.

He felt something behind him. A quick glance. Nothing. *You're losing it, Leo. You are losing your mind. This is it.* Everything he worked for. The picture, in the safe, the source of it all.

He should finish what he started, and destroy it.

But then he thought of her face, of her lidless dark eyes, that bore through him, the scream that drowned him.

She wasn't real.

But what if the photo wasn't what anchored her?

What if it was the only thing protecting him?

She would come back. She would shriek at him forever and show him everything she knew.

He couldn't burn it. He would keep it, protect it. For now. He would wait. He would return to work. It would be okay, be all right, be normal again.

He pulled himself off the floor, his body aching. He went to turn off the light. His finger touched the switch. A simple motion and blessed darkness would return.

Her eyes

He couldn't, not tonight. He would sleep with it on. He would shut them off tomorrow night, after everything faded, just a little.

The bed was there, soft and cool. The pillow embraced him. He laid down and focused on nothing, his body empty after being so full.

The visions were still there, everything she showed him. Charlie's grin and his gleaming eyes served as burnt negatives on the inside of his eyelids.

Leo closed his eyes, his bedroom bright, and tried to sleep.

He failed.

8

Leo stared at the camera, the red light burning his eyes. A pot of coffee had only stymied his exhaustion. The sweat was working through his makeup.

Leo was losing his mind.

Leo had laid asleep for hours, downing twice the recommended dosage of sleep aids. Nothing worked. He buried his head under the pillow, but every noise made him look for Truth, and when he closed his eyes the visions she gave him flashed behind his eyelids.

The pre-show rundown was nonsense. The words fell apart in his ears and the text on the page was unreadable. He stared at the paper. His script, containing the information on the pre-records and John's segment, was gibberish. Nothing was there except her eyes, flashes of the visions from last night.

He nodded when appropriate, watching Warren, but all the people at the table blinked in and out. Their eyes were gone, replaced by the dark holes of Truth's visage. He looked away from them, but they all were monstrous, mutated versions of themselves, or their mouths changed into Charlie Collins' awful grin.

"Leo?" asked Warren, staring at him.

"Yes?" asked Leo, looking up at Warren's face, then back down. He was Trevor now, blood bubbling out of his mouth as he was choked to death, strangled in the swamp by an anonymous killer.

"I asked if you're okay with John's segment," said Warren.

"Yeah, it's great," said Leo.

"Are you okay, Leo?" asked Warren.

Leo couldn't look at him. Trevor's eyes stared back at him. His wife will never know what happened.

"Yeah, I'm fine," said Leo. "Let's get to work."

He could feel all their eyes, but he couldn't look at them. They judged him. They didn't understand. She was here, she was in all of them. Their eyes were hers.

The camera was on him then, and he was falling apart. He tried to follow the teleprompter and the script.

———,..weigHE—__gegDIED
—][]kkFORtteeettYOU—

He could do this. *Focus, Leo.* Force her out of your mind. Push out the visions. Light danced in his vision and the dark circles of her eyes crowded him. The crew was silent, the camera pointed at him. They watched him. *She* watched him.

The teleprompter was unreadable, and she was there, her face, and she opened her mouth to scream at him.

"No!" said Leo, squeezing his notes in his hands. He shielded himself.

He looked back at the screen. She was gone. The words reappeared, full of gibberish and invective. They accused him.

"Are you all right, Leo?" asked Warren, his voice ringing out from the darkness behind the lights. Leo thought of Trevor's face. He remembered Trevor's eyes going blank as he died.

"Yeah, I'm okay," said Leo, straightening up his papers. A drop of sweat ran down his nose and landed on top of them, staining them.

He focused on his breathing. Leo closed his eyes and took a breath. *You're stronger than them, Leo, stronger than her.* He opened them.

She was there again, on the screen, and she screamed at him, her lamprey mouth opening wide.

He shrieked.

.

He was two glasses of scotch deep when Warren came into his office. The lights were on, and he wanted to leave, to get away from the stench of shame that filled the air. He had nowhere to go. His home was dangerous and full of *her.*

"What is going on with you, Leo?" asked Warren, walking in without knocking. "Is it the booze?"

Leo mustered his courage and glanced up at Warren. Mercifully, he looked himself.

"This is the only thing keeping me sane," said Leo. He

downed the glass and poured himself another. It was expensive scotch to not taste, but he needed it. Maybe. Truth had retreated after he screamed in the studio. The lights and visions receded.

"You need to take a break," said Warren. "You've been losing it, Leo. The blowup at John. Your performance the past couple days. You're struggling."

"I can't stop," said Leo. "John will have my job. I don't miss days. I can't. People trust me."

Warren looked at him, and sat down, a rarity for Warren. He was always on his feet, constantly moving.

"You're cracking, Leo," said Warren. "You've done this for years, with no breaks. The Truth is a behemoth, but that pressure is too much for anybody. Even you. Every man has a breaking point, and this is yours. I've seen it before. The booze has been a release valve for a long time, but it's not working anymore. That's clear. You need a vacation."

"You can't do this," said Leo, but he could hear his own voice. It sounded weak. He was Leo Price, goddamnit. He looked at Warren, and his face was the same one he knew and trusted. Concern was the only thing he read.

"I'm not making you do anything," said Warren. "This is only my advice, that you take a week or two off, relax, unwind, disconnect. Recharge, and return fresh. You'll be better for it, and so will the show. A break will give you new ideas and energy."

Energy. He was so tired. He looked at the drink, picked it up, put it down. Was Warren right?

"If you go on like this, you won't be taking a break voluntarily," said Warren. "I'll have to pull you, and John will have your spot permanently, because performances like today's cannot continue. The network won't understand it. You know how they work. You take some time off and rebound like only you can. Give them a chance to miss you."

Leo waited for Truth to interrupt. The visions would return to dominate his mind. They didn't come. Was all this overwork? This pressure to perform, this burden he refused to let go of.

He had seen Truth the night before, he was sure.

Or did he imagine it all? He looked at the scotch again. The stress, the booze, the lack of sleep, it was all getting to him. The picture was the final straw. It could drive any man to see things. Leo simply filled in the gaps. He made up a story in his head, a grandiose vision of the truth, and a harbinger to deliver it.

Was it real? Or was he losing his mind, under so much strain he cracked?

Warren was right. He needed a break, or he would lose the show. He would rest. He would get away. He would exorcise Truth.

A doubt lingered, deep within. What about Trevor? What about him missing, and the voice he had heard, the one that had crept into his life?

Leo pushed it aside, forced it into the hollow numbness the scotch burnt inside him.

"You're right," said Leo, finally. "I'll take some time."

Warren smiled, a slim smile, barely recognizable. "Great," he said.

"Over a thousand shows," said Leo.

"It's a big number," said Warren. "Unparalleled, especially on a show like ours. I should have stepped in earlier. But you were too good, Leo."

"I still am," said Leo.

"You are," said Warren. "And don't worry. I'll be here. I won't let them replace you. No matter how much John wants the job." Warren stood up. "Take a week. Go somewhere nice. Forget about it all. I'll manage everything here."

"You'll smooth it out with the network?" asked Leo.

"I'll make it work," said Warren. "You're doing research. Big project. Something like that."

"You're a good man," said Leo. "Where would I be without you?"

"Up shit creek, that's where," said Warren. "Now go. Take care of yourself."

It was strange being home so early in the day, back before lunchtime.

There were no more visions, no more dark eyes staring at him from the corners of his vision. It was all the proof Leo needed. Evidence of the effects of deep stress. Nothing more.

He packed, throwing clothes into a suitcase, still not knowing where he would go.

His eyes flitted to the photos on the wall, the only photo hanging of him and Diana. Early in their marriage, them at the beach house, the housewarming party. It was their dream. They had realized it, they had achieved it, noises in the night be damned. They were happy then. They spent so much time there. It was a refuge. And then everything fell apart.

He would go back there. Not to the house, but to the beach. The white sand, the clear air. It would straighten him out. It was what he needed.

He went online, found an Airbnb and booked it for a

week. A dozen miles from their old house.

Leo finished packing, throwing in the stack of books in his to-read pile. No computer, no social media. He would read. He would stare at the ocean. He would recharge like Warren said. He felt better already. He'd be himself again and Truth would disappear.

He uncovered his red Corvette. He'd ride with the top down. Too beautiful a car to not use for so long. He threw everything in the trunk, and he was ready to go.

No, not quite. Something stuck in his mind.

He went back into the house, beelining to his office. He slid the painting aside, revealing the safe.

Leo stared at it for a moment and then opened it. There was any number of things inside he could use on the trip, but there was only one thing he needed, and it was right on top.

The picture. He grabbed it off the top and tucked it into a pocket. Leo closed it and returned to his car, locking the house behind him.

He reversed out of the driveway, gunning the powerful motor as he left his neighborhood. Leo drove toward the beach, only a couple hours away, the wind whipping by him. The lack of sleep wasn't affecting him. He felt as strong as ever.

Leo didn't think about why he brought the picture with him. If he did, he would have realized the cognitive dissonance its presence required. He would have realized that it was the very thing he was trying to get away from. The thought would have broken him.

The crack already present in his mind would have widened, and he would fall inside. Because he knew deep within why he brought it with him. Because of his fear, because of the realization he made earlier, of why he never destroyed it, even when he wanted to.

He understood that the picture was how Truth found him, why she targeted him. And it was the only reason she let him live.

9

The barista smiled when he placed his order at the cafe on the beach. Leo's cup said "LIAR" on it. He was too tired to muster any outrage.

"Always great to meet a fan," he said, as he grabbed it and left, not looking back.

Rain fell on the mostly empty beach, a few stragglers walking and no one swimming. The house was nice. It was newly built. Leo sat on the patio, staring out at the ocean and sipping on his coffee. The water sprawled out before him. He loved it, the reassuring crash, its unassailable nature. It persisted.

He pulled the top book off of the stack he brought with him. It was Diana's latest, about the present and future of green energy and its legislation. He read all of her books. He never told her that. They talked rarely anyway, now that the kids were grown up, no real co-parenting left to do. Aside from an emergency loan, or just once, a call for career advice from Alex, Leo's parenting days were over.

He missed Diana. He had wanted to make it work, help their marriage survive, but it was impossible, untenable. The pistol was the first decision that set them at odds. The kids were older then, teenagers, but still living at home. She didn't want it in the house with them. He yelled, bellowed like only he could, about gun control, and protection, and safety. He forced his way to victory in the argument, another in a long line over the years.

He had felt good winning, but he knew now it was one more tally in Diana's mind, a loss she ceded not because he was right, but because she was not willing to burn down their marriage over it. But they mounted.

The Truth was the beginning of the end. He loved the show, still did, but she resented what it was, what *he* was while hosting. That the man he became on screen didn't leave when he left the studio. Leo brought it home with him. He turned into that persona.

She had blindsided him. It was obvious, looking back. He couldn't see it then, too busy with The Truth, caught up in the excitement. Ratings were through the roof then. His name was everywhere. It was intoxicating.

"What?" he asked.

"I've filed for divorce," she said. "Today."

He was watching the show. He paused it, his face on the TV stuck in a dumb grimace.

"I—" he said. "What? Why?"

She was calm, collected, rehearsed. He couldn't find his

bluster then. She had knocked it out of him.

"A lot of reasons, Leo," she said. "You're not who I married. You've become a different man, one I'm not interested in sharing my life with."

"The kids," he said. "They—"

"They already know," she said. "They both want to live with me. They'll both be gone soon, anyway."

His heart hurt. He pushed back tears, blinked his eyes. *Don't show weakness, Leo.*

"Can't we work this out?" he asked, staring up at her. "I can—"

"This is not a negotiation, Leo," she said, her voice soft. "It's over. You should contact your lawyer. I'm packing up my things and staying at a hotel for the time being. Please leave me to it."

She walked away, and he sat there, his show paused. He stared at himself, the set new, a graphic on the screen, about some 9/11 truther. He remained there and listened to the rustling upstairs as Diana packed her bags and left.

He had told the lawyers to give her what she wanted. She had been reasonable. She didn't want to hurt him.

Alex and Jennifer had moved in with her after she settled down. He hadn't asked them why they lived with her. He hadn't engaged with the divorce at all. The show was only getting bigger, and better. He negotiated a new contract, and then he had more money than he would ever need.

He bought the Corvette.

Alex was twenty-five now, married. Worked for Buzzfeed, and was writing his first book. Leo was proud of him and happy that he called him for career advice before he committed. He was a journalist, like his mom and dad.

Jen still wouldn't talk to him. He had blown up at her after she dropped out of school and moved out west. Diana told him she was doing well, waiting tables and making art, surviving.

He was a good father. He had provided for his kids, just like Diana. He was always louder, first to discipline. Of course they liked Diana more. The gun was to protect *them*.

He had done what he needed to defend them. It had all changed with the show. They didn't understand. The pressure to perform, every day. It was all for them.

That wasn't true, Leo.

He knew it was a lie. The work brought its own rush. The success got him the recognition he sorely craved. Years of writing and digging, of pouring his blood onto the page had given him little. He had gotten some shoddy awards, and modest pay, and no respect. They would appreciate him now. Leo had forced their hand.

He finished the coffee. He switched to the bottle of twelve-year-old Scotch.

The cost was more than his marriage, or seeing his kids every day. It was "LIAR" written on his cups. It was college students spitting on him. It was his house vandalized, his tires slashed. He had installed cameras and lights outside. Never caught anything but raccoons. They hated him.

Fuck 'em.

Leo grimaced at the initial sip of the scotch, but it warmed him anyway. He put down Diana's book and walked down to the water.

The sand was cool, the clouds thick and gray overhead, the shore deserted. He reclined on the ground, bottle squeezed between his fingers. The sea roared in and out. He drank and drank.

Their first evening at the beach house, before the restless night, had been lovely. They had moved in all their stuff during the day, both of them exhausted. Then it was dark and they laid on the sand, drinking. They had stared at the sky, listening to the waves.

They said nothing, just enjoying getting there, finally. They made love on the beach, in the dark, soft, tired, clumsy. They had picked sand off themselves for days. It was what they had worked for.

Gone now.

"It's still within reach," said Diana, next to him, her long blond hair piled around her face.

"Diana?" he asked.

"We can have it again," she said. "Quit television. Be a journalist again."

"I—I can't do that," he said. "I'm Leo Price, the show depends on me—"

"Shh," she said, and she kissed him. Her warm, soft lips touched his, and he returned it. Impossible to resist her. It always was.

They kissed, and their hands caressed each other, and then she was on top of him, her hips grinding on him, and he was hard, and insane, overwhelmed by her. She was naked then, and she pulled off his pants, and he was inside her. They were in broad daylight, someone would see, it doesn't matter, nothing matters. Except this.

She rode him, and he stared up at her, at her dark eyes. Nearly black, they were so dark.

Diana's eyes were hazel, a spectacular almost-gold never replicated.

This wasn't Diana and then the orbs grew wide, wider, wider still, darkening, a blackness, a darkness that swallowed up the light, her hair turning the color of soot, her skin pale white, her mouth expanded, lamprey eel and row after row of teeth and she *screamed*

He was in a familiar hallway, with red carpet and the idyllic wallpaper. *No, not here.*

He was alone in the corridor. No holding hand, no rictus grin, no gleaming eyes. The door at the end of the hall pulled at him.

He didn't know how, but it called to him, a siren's song. He walked toward it.

Leo looked down in his palm, and he saw it. A digital camera, big and clunky and expensive. He couldn't see that familiar smile because it was *his.*

He had to keep walking, couldn't halt his inevitable arrival. Every step got him closer, and he could hear the noise inside, the group of men, staring, leering.

He *was* Charlie Collins, and he was heading toward the room, inexorably. He could feel the grin on his face, and then he was at the door, and it was open, and he was there.

The show had begun already, Fred on top of Barbara. He closed the door behind him, shifting between the guys, some close, next to the bed, others leaning against walls. Some whispered between themselves, some laughed, and a few yelled at the pair, Fred thrusting into her. He saw their faces, and he knew so many of them. Judges, senators, lawyers. All men of power. No women aside from Barbara.

Leo could feel the smile on his face widen, felt himself bring up the camera to his eye, taking a picture, and another, and another. His heart was racing, a deep feeling of nervousness in his stomach. It was only the beginning of the night, but it thrilled him.

Please, no more, please. Truth. Please take me out of here.

He walked around the room, snapping dozens of pictures, of every angle, close and far. His vision spun away, toward the assembled men, who all stared. He turned, back toward the poor child, and Barbara. She moaned.

But it wasn't Barbara anymore. It was her, the creature that haunted him, that followed him. Truth.

She was underneath the kid as he thrust into her. Her hollow, dinner plate eyes open wide, staring through Frederic, staring through *everything*, into him.

Time extended, lengthened, the scene lasting minutes, hours, days, as Leo stalked around the room as Charlie, his erection throbbing in his pants, taking pictures, as Truth stared at him, her circular mouth opening wider and wider.

He couldn't stop.

And then he was on the beach again, the sun peeking out from behind the clouds above, shining in his face, the half empty bottle of scotch next to him. He sputtered and sat up. He was wet. He reached down, to the crotch of his pants, moist and damp. A wave of revulsion tore through him, and he threw up, the booze burning up his throat, out of his mouth and nose. He tilted over, forcing it out of him, into the sand.

He buried it and scrambled to his feet, his body aching. Still no one around.

He would shower, clean himself, and eat, get something in his stomach that wasn't coffee or booze. It would do him well. He needed to move, to lose *her.* A faint sound echoed over the waves crashing, over the unmovable, unassailable ocean. It was quiet, in sync with the ebb and flow of the water, but he heard it. It was unmistakable.

She had followed him here, to the beach. Hours from home. There was no losing her.

The shower and food would help. *It was just a nightmare, Leo.*

He retreated to the rental house, looming over the dunes. The water crashed behind him. The soothing noise of the ocean had accompanied his writing for years.

The waves crashed onto the beach, but all he heard was her scream.

<h1 style="text-align:center">10</h1>

Someone was watching Leo Price. He knew it.

The grocery store was empty in the gloomy afternoon. Leo paced around, pushing his cart, filling it with whatever caught his eye. Junk food, sushi, ice cream, boxed dinners, frozen chicken tenders. He noticed the man in the freezer section the first time, as Leo looked at the selection of frozen pizzas.

The man carried a basket with a few things in the bottom. He wore a Nationals baseball cap, a pair of jeans, and a t-shirt. Leo only saw a portion of his face.

He recognized his ring, though. A Washington College alumni ring. Leo had gone there, had met Diana there.

He noticed the ring earlier, at the cafe. A man, reading his newspaper, also waiting for his coffee. Couldn't see his face.

It's a coincidence, Leo. It's a small beach town. There are only so many places to be. She was affecting him, making him paranoid. Don't draw others into it.

He lingered inside, taking more time than normal. He stared at the flowers for sale and browsed the pharmacy. Leo kept his head on a swivel as he threw bottles of vitamins in his cart without looking at them.

Nothing, the man was gone, Leo wandering alone under the stark, cold lights of the store. Even the echoes of her scream were absent. No one followed him. He needed food and sleep.

You slept on the beach and she was there

He checked out. He would walk back, he would eat, he would doze off on a sofa.

"Are you Leo Price?" asked the young male cashier. He was blond, a smirk on his face.

"Yes," said Leo. He would lie, usually. Too many arguments with liberal retail employees. Too tired, his brain sluggish.

"Huge fan," he said, leaning slightly toward Leo. There was no one else within a hundred feet.

"Oh really?" he said. "Thank you. I appreciate it."

"That exposé you did on Obamacare really opened my eyes," he said. "Back in the day. Convinced me to take my family off of it."

This kid has a family?

"Your family?" asked Leo.

"Oh yeah," he said. "My three kids, my wife, even my parents. Got them off of it. Too dangerous, easy decision. Don't want them killing me in the hospital just because it's cheaper. My sister was screaming at me last Thanksgiving about my kids. She's one of them snowflakes you talk about, and I showed her that clip on Youtube, and it made her so angry, I laughed and laughed, she couldn't handle seeing the truth right in front—"

The kid kept talking, about his sister, about the other people here at the store, who don't understand it, don't get it, on and on, about various segments from The Truth. He stared at the boy, hearing none of what he said. The kid's eyes furrowed, spittle flying off his lips as he launched invective after invective about his family, his friends, all these sheep—

You did that, Leo

A whisper in his ear. He looked behind him. Nothing there, the empty store, the smile of a celebrity he didn't recognize from a magazine he thought failed. Gum, and candy bars. Batteries and flashlights.

He turned around and she was there. Truth loomed over him. The kid had vanished, subsumed by her.

"No," he said, not a yell or a scream, but a small exhalation, not loud enough for anyone to hear. He fell backward, covering his face. He couldn't revisit that hallway, please no more screaming.

He cowered behind his cart, scurrying backward into the next cashier stall, his hands up. She followed him here, she was everywhere, there was no escape.

"Mr. Price?" asked the kid. "Are you ok?"

He dropped his defenses and opened his eyes. He had squeezed them tight against her. It was just the cashier. He stood there, staring at him.

"Sorry, kid," he said, standing up, rushing, his face red,

his vision swimming. He threw the plastic bags into his cart. "I've got to go."

He kept talking behind him, but Leo wasn't listening. He pushed his cart out of the sliding doors, looking for the Corvette. Where had he parked?

The ring again. The man, sitting on a bench outside the store, eating a sandwich purchased inside, staring at his phone. The same ring, the same man. Waiting for him.

There was no doubt now. Someone was keeping tabs on him. Leo wanted to abandon his cart, advance on him. Question him.

But what would he get? Nothing. Of course they were watching him. He couldn't run away or hide from this. Trevor, the photo, it wouldn't just vanish because he took a vacation. He was a target as long as he had that picture.

He saw the Corvette, bright and red despite the gloom. Not like he was hard to find driving that around town. Anyone could hear it, a mile away.

There was no escape. He stopped at the liquor store again on the way back to the house.

Leo ate, but more so, he drank, staying in a stupor the rest of the day.

He sat on the recliner, in the television's glow, pouring himself neat whiskeys from the moment he returned. The wind picked up outside, and it buffeted the building, a storm rolling in, the ocean churning.

The liquor warmed him and exhaustion hit him hard. He dozed, his head falling against the cushion. The weariness overwhelmed the paranoia, the anxiety, the fear. His body wouldn't run anymore. He was out of gas.

She was waiting for him when he closed his eyes. Her

scream remained there. He jolted awake and drank more. He watched game shows. Any distraction was welcome.

The floor creaked above him on the second story of the home. He waited, and it groaned again, hollow, slow thumps above his head.

She was here. He knew it. She was taunting him, picking at him.

"What do you want from me?" he yelled, his words slurring, his loud voice echoing through the house. "I can't do anything! They'll kill me. They'll ruin me."

There was no response, but the floodgates opened. He stood up, spilling whiskey as he yelled at the ceiling.

"That damned picture! Why that picture? Why me? It was twenty years ago! I'm sorry for those children, I'm sorry for that pain, but there are worse things that happen every day! I should know, I have to ignore them. You don't chase *them*. You don't burrow into their minds, and keep them awake. *You* let them continue! You let them serve us. I'm just a TV host!"

He pulled the printout from his pocket, shook it at the sky, crumpled in his fist. He realized he was crying.

"Please," he said, looking back down. "Let me sleep. Just one night."

The house returned his plea with silence.

He sat down, unfolding the paper, staring at it. It hadn't changed, but it did nothing to him now. He had seen so much more than a bad picture on printer paper.

John's voice sprang from the TV.

"—there is no debate in my mind that the President is doing exactly what this country needs," he said, Leo looking up at the television, The Truth on the screen. "He's doing some much-needed pruning to a nation that has grown unruly for years and years. And I applaud him for it."

He turned to the second camera. "And now, for our new investigative piece about the true dangers of vaccines. Not autism, but cancer."

John was a natural, with no awkward breaks, seamless transitions, and perfect delivery of both news beats and monologues. His voice was low and powerful, and he projected without effort. He was ideal. He looked at home in front of the camera. Leo watched the rest of The Truth, the picture still in his hand.

John was better than him. He saw it now as clear as day. He was faster, more handsome, and able to move between topics easily. It continued and the jealousy was replaced by a deep ache of obsolescence. Leo was the old model. He remembered Warren's words, talking about him in the past tense. Would his position be waiting for him when he came back? Was this just an extended audition for the golden boy?

The show proceeded. A short news beat about reverse racism, and then job loss among white males.

It didn't matter. The picture would kill him, somehow. It fluttered into his lap. He would die, his body wasting away, some anonymous hitman murdering him a swamp, like Trevor. Truth, the wraith, was here, waiting to pounce on him. She wouldn't even answer him.

A commercial, and then a feature story on gun control. A gun owner was being interviewed, his face filling the screen. It was full of anger and vitriol. He had a rifle in his hand, wrapped tight around the stock, and with every word emphasized, he thrust his weapon forward.

It continued. Segment after segment of angry men, of

outrage, of perceived and imagined slights, of carefully crafted tribalism.

This was wrong. The show had ended by now. Still, the segments rolled on, with John segueing between them, a smile plastered on his face. More anger, more venom. Produced to elicit the most emotion, to guide the viewer, to dose them in this bestial rage. They would come back for more tomorrow.

It got louder and louder. The remote was useless, and Leo found himself suspended in his chair, unable to get up, helpless to shut his eyes. They were frozen open, absorbing the poison pouring out of the screen.

It cut to the studio, and it was him, now. John was gone. It was Leo in control, at his peak. Composed, cool, delivering the news, transitions, everything. Perfect.

But his words—something was wrong. Leo watched himself, and he wasn't speaking, merely barking, yelling gibberish, bellowing raw animosity at the camera. It cut to another segment, on location, and the people there did the same, spitting, sputtering rage, globs of saliva flying out of their mouths. They were beyond language, fury the only thing left. It went on.

He couldn't stop it, the stream of anger, of disgust, pouring into his eyes, he could feel it filling him like Truth filled him with her screams, and now he understood.

He knew why *he* was given the picture, why Truth would not let him retreat or relent.

He was responsible. As much as anyone. He distributed poison every day. Misinformation. Propaganda. Toxic words that disseminated hatred. The balance was off. He broke the scale, creating more than his fair share. He needed to find the truth again.

And Truth had no limit.

The television was off and he could move, the picture still in his hand. He folded it up and tucked it back into his pocket. The floor creaked above him.

He couldn't face her again. The encounter would kill him. He fled.

It was dark now, the sun gone, the wind and rain howling. He ran, his shoes filling with water, his body soaked. His chest heaved with exertion, down the road that stretched up and down the coast. He knew she would follow, but he didn't care. Hell was behind him.

Cars passed him in the night, torrents hitting him, shot out from under their tires. He sprinted.

His feet pounded the wet road, no thought entering his head except escape.

Leo ran through the rain and found himself knocking on a familiar door, one he had walked through countless times. He knocked, his body broken and his mind fragile.

Diana answered.

"Help," he said. It was all he had.

Confused, her eyes read him.

"Come in."

11

Diana grabbed a towel from somewhere and wrapped it around him. She had changed the design inside, with new furniture and colors. It was still *their* house, however you disguised it. He pulled the cloth close, drying his hair.

"You look like warmed over shit, Leo," she said, sitting down across from him. "Why the hell are you here?"

Leo had put on weight since the divorce, no matter how many miles he ran. Diana looked the same, the same blond Amazon he had married twenty odd years ago. The last time he saw her was at Alex's graduation. They were friendly, but not friends.

"I don't know," he said. "I'm losing my mind. I haven't slept in three days. I've been seeing things. Hallucinations, nightmares. Vivid. I'm being followed. There was a man today, around town, with a Washington College ring, everywhere I was."

"Slow down," she said. "When did it start?"

"I got a lead," he said. "A big one."

"Really?" she asked. "Something real?"

"Yes," he said. "Well, I don't know. I think so. It started there, and everything has unraveled since."

"What is it?" she asked.

"I can't tell you," he said.

She sighed, rolled her eyes. "You come crawling in out of the rain, looking like a fucking zombie, smelling like whiskey, interrupt my writing, and you can't tell me."

"I want to, but I can't—" he said.

"Then why are you here? Why did you come to me?" she asked. "I promise, it's not because of my bedside manner."

"You're all I've got," he said.

She stared at him, struggling to read him. She knew when he was hiding something, even from himself. It's why he had loved her. At first.

"Then tell me," she said.

"I can't," he said, his voice hard.

"Bullshit, Leo," she said. "I can't—"

"It's dangerous, Diana," he said.

"So you're trying to protect me?" she asked. "I've seen the worst of it, Leo. You know that. Hell, back in the day—"

"Someone's dead, Diana."

"What?" she asked.

"They killed him. They killed my lead," he said. "They dragged him out into the swamp, and strangled him in the muck."

"How do you know that?" she asked.

"I told you," he said. "I can't."

She looked at him again, her gaze softer. She got up and went to the kitchen. He glanced around, his eyes flitting from photo to photo, hanging on the wall. Alex at his graduation. A picture of Jen he had never seen before, of her embracing the Hollywood sign. Them all together, the kids very young. Diana hadn't remarried, and he saw no trace of co-habitation. Did she date? He didn't want to know.

When they broke up, he had run through a string of women. All of them were insubstantial, attracted to his fame and rising star. He knew many men who dated younger women, who reveled in their youth and the age difference. Dating them didn't make him feel young. It made him feel ancient.

No romance since, and no real desire for it. He focused it into his work. Put everything there.

Diana came back, with warm tea. He sipped it, and it warmed his throat and belly.

"Why are you out here?" she asked.

"Warren pushed me toward a break. A vacation. I was losing it at tapings. John Stahlbock is subbing in for me. I thought the beach would do me good. The stress and the drinking—" he said. "It followed me here."

"And you're being tracked?" she asked.

"Yes," he said. "That man was real, and he was nearby everywhere I went in town. They're keeping tabs on me. He warned me."

"Who did?" asked Diana.

"Warren," he said. "Someone from above knew it was coming and instructed him to stay away. He said the same to me. I didn't realize. I thought I was safe. I thought we were safe—"

"Leo, tell me," she said. "I'm a grown up. What's the story?"

He looked at her again, and her golden eyes stared back. Soft now. Few had seen them like that. He reached into his pocket and pulled out the folded picture, slightly soggy. He handed it to her.

She unfolded it, staring at it.

"That's Barbara Collins," she said.

"You got it a lot faster than I did," he said.

"And that's—Simonson?" she asked. "A bunch of other people. Swinging? Cuckold fetish?"

"The man, the kid, on top of her," he said. "Frederic Collins. The photograph was shot by Charlie Collins himself."

"Jesus," she said.

"Yeah," he said. "Tip of the iceberg."

"What else is there?" she asked. "More pictures? Video?"

"I have nothing else," he said.

"Only the picture?" she asked. "It's something, but it's not enough."

He finished the tea. It settled in Leo. He was warm and wanted to pass out. She'd be waiting for him. He knew it. She wouldn't let him rest.

He would tell her.

"This is where I go insane," he said.

Diana raised an eyebrow, her bullshit detector on high alert.

"It was right after I got the photo," he said. "The same night. First, a call from my source's number, warning me away. It wasn't his voice. Someone else. A fixer. He said it was a courtesy. Later, I had a nightmare. I saw my source get tortured. Dragged out into the swamp. Killed. She was there."

"It lingered the next day," he said. "And it's gotten worse. I saw her, all of her, last night. She showed me so much more than that picture. I can't remember it all, only bits and pieces, fragments. But the Collins adopted eight children from around Africa, boys and girls. And I know that Fred isn't the only victim."

"You keep referring to a woman, showing you things," she said. "Who? Who is she?"

"Truth," he said.

"Truth?" she said.

"Yes," he said. "She *is* Truth. Three days now. Without sleep, without rest. She's giving me—visions. Visions of rape and death. I can't take it anymore."

Diana furrowed her brow, and grabbed her phone, typing something in.

"Do you recognize the name Jean-Léon Gérôme?" she asked.

"No," he said. "You know I'm bad with names."

She flipped the screen around and showed him a painting on it. It was a naked woman, emerging from a well, a look of torment on her face.

"How about this?" she asked.

"I don't recognize it," he said. "I like it. Powerful."

"Gérôme was an artist. This was his. Truth Coming Out of Her Well to Shame Mankind," said Diana.

"That's not her," he said. "There's nothing beautiful or pure about this thing. The only part I recognize is her rage."

"I'm not saying she is," said Diana. "I'm saying that you saw this painting somewhere, and you created her, Leo.

You've internalized your guilt about your program and drowned it in whiskey for seven years. With no vacation the whole time. In a position I do not like, but one that is no doubt stressful."

"I don't feel guilty about The Truth," he said. "It's an achievement. I've topped the ratings for months, years straight."

"Don't try and sell me on what you sold yourself," she said. "I know you, Leo. Better than anyone else. And I'm sure you've convinced yourself that your show is harmless entertainment. But you used to peddle the truth. And now it's snake oil."

The television, the venom, the fury that poured out from him, to him. She was right. It was killing him.

"You need to reckon with that," she said. "You've put it off for far too long."

He *had* seen Truth. Those visions, those hallucinations. They weren't the product of his mind. Truth was real. She was here somewhere, watching him. He looked at Diana. She sat across from him, confident in her diagnosis. Her eyes betrayed her worry for him. She didn't believe him.

"What do I do?" he asked.

"It started with that picture," she said. "Maybe something inside wants you to chase that story, like the old days. Despite the danger."

"I'll get fired," he said. "And I didn't dream up the missing persons report filed for my informant."

"It's a risk," she said. "But when wasn't it?"

She handed him back the printout, and he tucked it away again.

"You want my advice?" she said. "Follow the truth. Investigate the story. You were always good at it. And stop drinking."

He paused. Listening. No distant screams, no creaking floors.

"Can I crash here tonight?" he asked.

"Alex's room is the guest bedroom. I'll make up the bed. There's Chinese in the fridge if you're hungry." She turned to get the bed ready.

"Diana," he said, and she stopped, looked back.

"You're free to help with the story," he said. "Just like old times."

She smiled. "Not my game anymore," she said. "You know I never liked it much anyways." She went upstairs. Leo's stomach growled. He was voracious, the junk food not tiding him over. He grabbed the takeout and ate it with his hands in front of the fridge.

Diana was back. "Bed's ready. I'll be working if you need me."

"Thank you," he said. "I mean it."

"I know," she said.

He plodded upstairs, his feet and eyelids heavy. Alex's room was at the end of the hall on the left. Everything that was Alex had been removed. The same bed his son once slept on was now covered with fresh sheets and blankets. He stripped to his underwear and laid down, cracking the door.

He could hear Diana's typing echo upstairs, the faint clack of her keyboard, bursts of writing and then silence.

Leo wanted to sleep, but he stared up into the darkness. The conversation with Diana circled in his head. Of course she didn't believe him. It was insanity. But it didn't change that it was true. Those visions were real. He knew that Charlie Collins pulled a young child down that long hallway to that accursed room at the end. The slick grin, his eyes looking down, the excitement in them. It had all happened.

It was the truth, and he would follow it. He would dig into Charlie Collins, he would find out the whole story. He'd shove it in their goddamn faces, position be damned. They couldn't deny him.

Threaten *his* life? He was Leo Price, goddamnit. They would pay. They would all pay. Pay the cost for hiding the truth. He would uncover everything.

And he'd stop drinking.

A moment of panic hit him. The picture. He got up, grabbed it from his pocket, and shoved it under his pillow. It was precious, invaluable.

Diana's typing click-clacked from downstairs and his eyelids fell. The dark, the warm tea, and the noodles in his stomach brought sorely needed comfort. The bed was soft. He closed his eyes, not waiting for Truth to attack or another terrible vision. The boiling tension he had felt for days was gone.

Diana typed, the house creaked, and Leo slept through the night.

12

The sun woke Leo up.

The house was quiet. A note downstairs.

*I'm gone for a few days. Take what you want from the kitchen.
Be careful.
Call if you need help.
Diana*

He left one in return.

*Thank you. Will let you know.
Leo*

He walked back toward his rental, his clothes shabby,

dry, ill-fitting from their soaking the night before. The picture was in his pocket.

He was refreshed. His body ached, but his feet didn't drag as he went down the main road. The ocean crashed in on his left from beyond the condos. He changed and showered when he returned. Cleaned. Dumped the remaining liquor down the drain, threw the bottles in the blue bin.

Leo stopped at the grocery store, the Corvette roaring down the highway. He grabbed enough food for the rest of his stay. Chicken soup, mashed potatoes, some bagged salads. A lot of soup, and Gatorade. The next couple of days would be rough.

Early on, the drinks were only to calm him down after late nights working a story, soothing frayed nerves after meeting sources. Alcohol served as social lubrication at times, to make people comfortable. As the years passed on, the booze became more regular. It was an easy way to cope with the pressure. But he never lost control, not with Diana or with Alex or Jen.

With them gone, there was nothing keeping him in check. Leo performed for millions of people every single night. They expected the best from him and he delivered it. There was cost. Cost in liters of scotch, of whiskey, of bourbon.

It had been twelve hours since his last drink. A few more and he'd be shaking. The clock was ticking.

He walked down the aisles, studying food as he passed. He checked his peripheral vision, looking down the aisle. No tails and no man with a Washington College ring. The market was active, but it was a lot of tourists, gearing up for one of the final summer weekends.

No one followed him, and he paid. He avoided the fan-boy employee. If his cashier recognized him, she didn't let on.

He found the only electronics shop in town, a big box store on its last legs. He bought a laptop and a tablet. They matched the models he left at home. He needed to work.

No stop at the liquor store.

Back to the rental.

He ate some chicken soup and made himself a little workstation on the dining room table.

He had a couple of hours before it would hit him. He worked.

He built the story.

Charlie Collins. Served as a Congressman, from Virginia. Long-tenured, old Republican. Well respected, served on many committees, and sub-committees. Faced no serious competition for re-election. Famed for "reaches across the aisle" over the years, reaching compromise on important bills. Never worked toward higher office, always deflected any attention or questions about running for President. No biological children. Adopted eight from various parts of Africa, of different ages. In conjunction with charity work donating to African causes, he and his wife Barbara retained stellar reputations. Died in 2005 from a stroke. Buried in Virginia.

Repeatedly raped and abused his adopted children. Took photos, and invited others in his circles to watch or partici-pate. **NO DIRECT EVIDENCE**

Barbara Collins. High school sweetheart of Charlie. Some say as integral as him in his rise to power and influ-ence in Washington, if not more so. Her parties were famous, with Barbara as the eminent hostess. More involved with charity work than Charlie himself. Lives in their home in Virginia, currently eighty-five years old.

Repeatedly raped and abused her adopted children. Invited others to watch or participate. **DIRECT PHOTO EVIDENCE**

Adam Simonson. Current Speaker of the House. Forty-five years old. Republican powerhouse, and rumored to be running for President in 2024. Steadily worked his way up through the state politics, to national, to Speaker. Steady progression. Has big friends, and big enemies. Certainly has influence on the network.

Watched rape and sexual abuse, and potentially participated. **DIRECT PHOTO EVIDENCE**

May have arranged for the death of Trevor Williams. **NO DIRECT EVIDENCE**

Leo's hands shook, and he noticed the sweat on his forehead. It would hit him hard soon. He built the story.

Frederic Collins. Adopted son of Charlie and Barbara Collins. Victimized by them, and potentially others. Lives in Maryland, a graduate of UM. Married, no children. Thirty-five years old.

Victim. And the first person he would interview.

Sweat was trickling down his back, and his stomach twisted inside. Leo swallowed the bile, taking a deep breath. It didn't help, and he ran to the bathroom. He vomited up the chicken soup.

He was sick for two days. He ate soup and crackers and sometimes threw them up. He laid in bed, soaking the sheets with sweat, rolling around in pain.

No hallucinations, no hysteria. Leo could handle the

suffering, as his body adjusted to life without alcohol. He slept poorly. He'd wake up to vomit, and try and keep some Gatorade down.

Then it passed. He was a wreck, but his head was clear, clearer than it had been for years.

He walked out on the beach, the early morning sun shining, and focused on the ocean, feeling the salty breeze. He listened hard, his eyes closed. He was feet away from where he fell asleep only days before, when he was visited by Truth. He stood, and waited, waited for a sign of her.

Nothing. The sea roared, but there wasn't a hint of Truth's brutal language.

He finished his research. He found addresses for all of the Collins' kids, and for Barbara herself. She was eighty-five and battling dementia. The last report had her only semi-coherent, and it's doubtful she'd cooperate if she even remembered anything. There was a chance of physical evidence. But it wouldn't come willingly.

Most of the children lived out of state, a couple out of the country. Frederic was the only one who stayed local. He would be first.

He still had four days of vacation at the beach. He considered going back early and forcing Warren's hand. Better not to. For anyone observing, he *was* resting, and doing exactly as he was told. Leo was being a good little boy. He was taking a break, and absolutely not putting his nose anywhere it didn't belong. The longer whoever was watching believed him, the easier time it would be to do his work. Truth's work.

He would look at the picture, hold it. He took pictures of it, and copied them to all his devices, to the cloud. Leo cursed his earlier stupidity. Another mistake like that would sink his investigation.

He hadn't known then, hadn't understood. Truth was trying to show him the path, the only way she knew how. She only spoke one language, and Leo just needed to learn it.

He didn't hear her, but he did feel her there. Her presence. There were no groans in the night, or nightmares, for that matter, but there was something there with him. She felt different now. The word "aura" made him angry, but it was the best way to describe it. It surrounded him. It *embraced* him.

So he relaxed and read and waited. He treated himself to some nice dinners. He ran on the beach in the morning and swam in the cooling Atlantic waters. He was alone, aside from Truth.

He went home and found his house ransacked, worse than he did himself in his rampage against Truth. Furniture was knocked over, destroyed in some cases. The refrigerator was tipped over, both fridge and freezer doors open, the contents ruined, rotting food left on the kitchen floor. Almost nothing was untouched.

His computers were gone, both his desktop and the laptop he took to work.

The safe was open, the painting in front of it destroyed. Everything inside was still there, his important papers and records. Not a single thing missing. Leo verified.

They had added an object to it, sitting right on top, unmistakable. He didn't understand at first. Then he realized, and his guts ached. Trevor. Trevor and his dumb internet handle.

The one thing on top was a black hat.

13

Leo knocked on John's open office door and peeked his head in.

"Leo," said John, stopping typing for a moment, and then starting back again. "Vacation treated you well?

"Yes," said Leo. "Sorted some things out."

"Good to hear," said John, not looking at him.

Leo stood there, peering in, silent. Time to swallow his pride.

"Can I help you?" asked John. "I've got work to do, and—"

"John," he said. "Do you want to join Warren and me for the production meeting?"

John stopped typing, looked at Leo.

"Is this a trick?" asked John.

"No trick," said Leo. "You did a good job in my absence. I was wrong before. I want to bring you in, give you more responsibility. Make us better."

Leo walked back into the studio, anxious nerves making his stomach hurt. Being away from the show for the first time in eight years. No more visions, no more hallucinations. The peace with Truth would make this easier. And with John taking a bigger role, Leo would have less to do.

He let Warren and John take the lead in the production meeting, nodding, agreeing to what they said, what they suggested. His mind was on Charlie Collins and the black hat that was left in his destroyed home.

Leo hadn't called the police. What would he tell them? Could he even trust them? He had picked up his house the night before, putting things back where they belong, no different from his own crazed rampage. He had thrown away the broken stuff. No loss.

They watched him, and no amount of warnings were enough. They had tried to scare him. Nothing was comparable to Truth. None of them could do what she did.

The meeting flew by, even with John asking questions of Warren. Warren answered them, with Leo chipping in as well. It was old hat to Warren. He had answered the same questions for Leo, so long ago, and someone before that, and before that.

John contributed some ideas for the general scope of the show and they considered them. He also pitched some new regular segments, but they tabled them for later. Leo was back, and that was the main focus. Even so, John was excited, enthusiasm bubbling up. Was Leo wrong about him, this whole time?

He pulled Leo aside after the meeting but before they filmed.

"You won't regret this," he said.

"Wasn't a thought," said Leo, lying. But he needed John, required him to pick up the slack Leo couldn't carry anymore. And he was just plain tired of being hated by him.

Leo sat behind the studio desk, squaring up his notes. No dancing black eyes in his vision, no screams of Truth. He was back on track.

"Welcome, once again, to The Truth! I'm Leo Price. Let's get to it."

Leo faced the camera, the first news item.

"The President has again raised Chinese tariffs. This comes weeks after the last round of trade discussion failed, with neither side willing to budge."

A clip of the President at a podium, answering a question about the tariff.

"A smart move by the President. We've criticized China's role in global commerce for a decade now, and finally someone is doing something about it. It will hurt, as prices increase, but it's only the lumps we should have taken long ago."

That's not true, Leo, and you know it. He doesn't know what he's doing. He's ruining people's lives, and you're helpi—

Leo blinked and pivoted to the other hard camera. A dull pit of ache in his stomach opened up.

"Another critic of the Me Too movement has come out with a strong statement decrying the feminist crusade, saying it divides men and women."

A clip of a famous actor plays. "It's a small group of people, I would say women, but it's men too, who want to start a gender war. They're using misinformation to pit women against men and spread mistrust and quite frankly, it's evil."

Back to Leo. "Strong words from an acclaimed actor. In such divisive times, I think we have to try and fight against any factions, any groups, that seek to separate us."

Three women, Leo. He's raped three women, abused twice that, denigrated so many more. Monster, inhuman, and YOU ARE HELPING HIM

The pain in his stomach swelled, and he pushed it down.

"Now a word from our sponsors."

The same prerecorded video plays, with Leo sitting in his home office. He's typing at his computer. He turns to face the camera, his voice speaking out.

"I'm no stranger to late nights and long days, as I try and break the latest story, or get in touch with sources across the globe. When I'm feeling run down, or need a burst of energy to keep me working hard, I reach for Dynamite Energy Formula, the newest and best energy shot from our friends over at Blasco."

He reaches for an energy shot and holds it up to the camera.

LIAR

"Dynamite Energy Formula packs vitamins, minerals, and nutrients into a two-ounce shot that will keep you awake and active throughout the day while giving your body everything it needs."

Leo downs the shot and smiles, and then puts it down and gets back to work.

The feed cuts to Leo at his news desk.

"Thank you again to Blasco and Dynamite Energy Formula for sponsoring and supporting the show. It wouldn't be possible without you," said Leo.

THIEF

"And now a word from senior reporter John Stahlbock, who did a fantastic job filling in for me. John," Leo said, and then John was on camera.

"Thanks, Leo, it was a pleasure," he said. "My feature today is about personal responsibility. We are seeing complaint after complaint about the worker's rights for mega-retailer Amazon. But we don't hear the other side of the story."

Leo watched the feed, as a handful of workers for Amazon each extolled the virtues of the company. They gave me a job when no one else would. Yeah, it's hard work, but I ain't complaining. I get plenty of time to go to the bathroom, don't know what they're talking about.

Every show, Leo. Every show is filled with lies, and you are King—

It was time for the closing monologue.

"I was gone for a week, my first break from the show in its seven years. It was refreshing, relaxing. John did a terrific job in my absence. It was also hard for me. I don't like taking time off. I've built this program, along with my crew and producer, and leaving it for any length of time is like leaving a child."

"But my vacation did help me realize what's important, and why I do it. It's easy to lose track of that, over the years. It all comes back to the title, why we called it that in the first place. The Truth. Pure, unadulterated. And despite what most people think, the truth is not always easy to find. It varies from person to person. People remember things differently, see things differently, presented with the same set of facts."

"And I used to resent that when I was a young man. I wanted life to be simple, to be black and white. I learned that the world is complicated, but the true notion of right and wrong, true and false always resonated. And I've lost sight of that over the years. Making this show is hard work, and keeps me busy, involved. I was missing the forest for the trees."

"My promise to you, the viewer, the loyal audience, is to not waver, not falter, and give you exactly what you need to hear."

"That's it for us today. Thanks for watching, and don't forget that this is The Truth!"

Leo walked back to his office, the crew wrapping up the show, the recordings already being sent to the editors, the great machine turning. The hollow ache in his stomach was still there. It would be there until it was done. Truth was right to hurt him.

It was a pain he would have to bear.

He looked at his small bar in the corner, the bottles of scotch and whiskey. Even looking at them made him feel sick.

Warren knocked and entered, their daily ritual starting again, just like normal.

"Good show today," said Warren. "No ring rust. Ace monologue."

"I meant every word," said Leo.

"No drink?" asked Warren, peering over his glasses.

"No," said Leo. "I might be done with it."

"Wow," said Warren.

"You were right," said Leo. "About everything. I was focusing on the wrong things. Too worried about John, about the show. I concentrated on myself. I'm ready to make the program something special again."

"That's exciting," said Warren. "I think with John on board with our production meetings, we'll have the chance to try new ideas, see how they work."

"That's exactly why I brought him in," said Leo. "There's no use fighting the tides. He's talented, we might as well use what we have."

They covered Warren's observations from the show, plus any notes they expected for the next day and a preview of tomorrow morning's meeting. He left Leo alone in his office.

He watched Warren go. He wouldn't be able to keep this up. The pain in his gut was dulling, but it would only get worse with time. Eventually, it'd override everything he was, and force him to quit the show.

But he needed it for now. It gave him cover, and enough clout to forestall the people fighting his investigation. He would need it when he interviewed Frederic Collins.

Truth would hurt him, and he would beg for forgiveness, and take his lumps. He was trying to pay down his ledger and breaking the Collins case would do it. But he needed to avoid the attention for now. Business as usual to the outside observer.

He grabbed the bottles of booze and shoved them all in his office trash can. Maybe the cleaning crew could make use of them.

He went home.

The house was normal today, untouched, unspoiled, as he left it that morning.

He studied his research from the week, formulating a plan, to build his case. He would start with Frederick. He was in the picture, direct evidence. He could have access to more and might be willing to help Leo to further along the investigation. He lived close, and Leo could visit him after work tomorrow.

He met him once before, long ago, when Fred was still a child. Had it already started, then?

It was at a Collins' party, the first and only time he went. With Diana. They were both young, fresh hires of the paper and an editor passed on his invitation to them. As fledgling reporters, they had needed the networking and the contacts.

Leo had hated the pomp, the clothes, everything. He rented a tuxedo, no money to buy or get one fitted, and it squeezed his waist all night. His neck didn't like ties either. He met people, ate the food, and tried to be polite. He succeeded, for the most part. Mostly because of Diana.

She was a natural at these events. She had looked beautiful in her simple black dress. Diana glided from conversation to conversation, easy enough to introduce herself, to find the people she already knew and expand her circle of contacts. Leo was forced to participate. She had told him beforehand that this was reporting, as important as any other part of the job.

And she had been right. But he still hated it. She had felt at home there, like he did out in the muck, in the shadows, meeting lowlifes and informants to get the leaks he needed to tell a story.

He had met Fred that night, along with all other kids. They all smiled when introduced, and shook his hand, and were perfectly polite, and disappeared soon after. Leo had thought little of it but he had also been busy being miserable in the company of all those rich assholes.

If he had looked, would he have seen a look of sadness in their eyes? Desperation? Terror? Or did Charlie hide that away too?

14

The picture thrummed in Leo's pocket as he knocked on Frederic Collins' door. Truth knew he was close.

He stood on the doorstep in the upper class suburban neighborhood. Fred's home was nearly identical to all the others within view. Three stories, a front porch, and a small lawn. The two bordering houses encroached on the house. Modern construction, meaning as cheap as possible.

His wife opened the door, olive skin and dark hair, beautiful. She was surprised to see him. Leo opted to not call ahead. He didn't know what Frederic's reaction would be, and the element of surprise would work in his favor. Fortune favors the bold.

"Hi, I'm Leo Price," he said, extending his hand to her. He smiled as genuinely as he could.

She shook it, a look of mild shock on her face, shifting to furrowed eyebrows.

"Angelica. I know who you are," she said. Hostile territory.

"I'm here to speak to Frederic," he said. "Is he available?"

"Can I ask why?" she asked. She didn't move from inside the door, guarding the entrance.

"I'm working on a book. My first," he said. "It's about Charlie and Barbara Collins. I was hoping to talk it over with Frederic, and their other children." It was the easiest and best cover story he came up with.

Her posture changed, opened. She slowly moved back, opening the door for him, her features softening.

"Come in," she said. "Let me ask Fred."

He waited in the hallway in the suburban home, as Angelica disappeared further into the house. It was full of pictures of the couple. All happy, all smiling.

She appeared again.

"Follow me," she said, and she led him into Fred's office, where Frederic sat in a chair next to a computer. He stood as Leo came in. He was bigger than in the picture, years of natural growth and another twenty pounds of muscle on top. Fred was incredibly fit. His polo shirt was snug in the shoulders and tight in the arms. He was bald now. His face was unreadable.

Still, seeing him up close, he was unmistakable as the person in the photo. Leo felt it pulse in his pocket.

"Mr. Collins," said Leo, extending a hand.

"Mr. Price," he said, grabbing and shaking with a firm grip. They sat down, another smaller chair pulled over closer to Fred.

"You have a lovely house," said Leo, smiling, trying to appear genuine.

"Thank you," said Frederic, the same smile reflected at him.

"Angel," said Frederic. "Could you close the door?"

She closed it. They were alone.

"I'm surprised to see you here," said Frederic. "Angelica says you're writing a book about my parents."

Yes," he said. "I—"

Fred raised two fingers, and Leo let him talk.

"Before you go any further," he said. "I don't know how comfortable I am about that. I've seen your show, Mr. Price, and I do not like it, to be blunt. If it represents what that book is, expect resistance from me, and my siblings."

"I understand," Leo said. "And I agree. And to be frank with you, I don't think I'll be doing The Truth much longer. By the time the book will be out, the program may still air, but I won't be attached. My producers have dissuaded me from pursuing it at all. But I've felt—a calling to Barbara and Charlie's story. I assure you, this will be closer to my old journalism. Just the facts. It's why I'm here, in person. I endured two hours of traffic to get here, after work. I intend to do right by your parents. If it's what it takes, I'll give you and your siblings first pass at it, after it is done."

"Is that right?" asked Fred.

Leo looked him in the eye. "I know what people think about me and about my show. They're largely correct. But I plan to tell the truth about your mother and father."

Fred eyed him and relented. "Ok," he said.

"Can I ask you some questions?" asked Leo. "To get started?"

"Sure," he said.

"May I record the conversation?"

"Sure."

"How old were you when you were adopted?" asked Leo. Start small. A baseline.

"Eleven."

"Do you remember your reaction when you got the news?"

"I was happy," he said. "The orphanage I lived in was poor, and life was hard. America was built up as a land of opportunity. As a fantastically rich place."

"Did you meet the Collins before they chose you?" Leo asked. "And did you have any idea who they were?"

"Yes, I met them," he said. "We knew of them. They had been there before. They had taken two children prior from the same orphanage. Max, and Sara. I didn't know them at the time."

"What was the adjustment process like, coming over, and living with the Collins?" asked Leo.

"It was hard. We lived in a mansion, with a maid. We had private tutors and expensive schools. I went from having nothing, no belongings, to having anything I wanted. It took me a while to understand that this wasn't normal, not even in America. I was so lucky."

Leo looked at him then, and saw that he believed what he said. No insincerity, no double-talk. He *believed* in his luck.

"Were you close to your parents?" Leo asked. "To either Barbara or Charlie?" *Draw him in.*

Fred paused.

"Closer to mother," he said, finally. "Father was always gone, constantly working. As I grew older and learned about the things he did, it made more sense. But mother was usually there, even if she was busy entertaining."

"He was there for the parties, though," said Leo. "I remember that."

"He was," he said. "You're right. He never missed one. Those parties."

"We met there," said Leo. "I only attended one, that I can recall, but we met."

"We did," said Frederic, nodding.

"You remember?" asked Leo. "You were so young."

"I do," he said. "Almost everyone. They—they stood out in my mind."

"They were important," said Leo. "Movers and shakers. If you wanted to be someone in Washington, you were at the Collins' banquets. Do you recollect the planning at all?"

"I never had much to do with it," he said. "The house was always busy as they approached, full of caterers, of florists. My parents, they must have spent over six figures on flowers over the years. It was so extravagant but so normal to them."

"Were you comfortable at the parties?" asked Leo.

"What do you mean?" asked Frederic.

"You kids stood out like a sore thumb. African children, in the middle of a bunch of white Americans. It wasn't strange to you?"

"That was my life, Mr. Price," he said. "I—we, were always the other, wherever we went. Even at home. But it wasn't odd. It was normal. I expected it."

"Did you ever feel used by your parents?" asked Leo, his eyes flitting up to Fred again, reading him.

"I don't know what you mean," he said.

"It was an allegation against Charlie, from his nastier

opponents," said Leo. "That he raised you kids for optics, as a publicity stunt. You were always something he could point at, to distract from a piece of unpopular legislation, or during a lull in an election year. To drum up support."

"I do not think—" he said, choosing his words. "That my parents adopted any of us because of political reasons."

Leo was getting closer. The picture was screaming in his pocket. He could feel Truth's presence. She pushed him, held him.

"You never felt like trophies?" asked Leo.

"I don't know, it was a long time ago," said Frederic. *LYING*

"Did you know about the secret rooms?" asked Leo.

"What are you talking about?" asked Fred, looking away.

"I heard rumors, still do," said Leo. "Of a second invite, a private one. A sub-set, the elite, your father's favorites. And they got to attend a special invitation-only group."

"I have no idea what you're talking about," said Frederic. "They were just parties."

HE WAS THERE

"Are you sure about that, Fred?" asked Leo, making eye contact.

Fred peered back, and the silence hung between them. The picture hummed.

"Why are you *really* here, Mr. Price?" asked Fred. Fred stared at him, his eyes dead. Leo's ruse would carry him no further.

Leo held his gaze and then reached into his pocket, pulling out the folded piece of paper. He handed it over to Fred, who grabbed it, unfolded it. He recognized what it was.

Fred's face softened, his eyes opening, wavering. Vulnerability, raw pain, and sorrow floated across them.

But just for a second, and then his facade was up again.

"How did you get this?" asked Fred.

"An anonymous source," said Leo. A dead man, Fred. He died for that picture.

"Why did you bring this to me?" he asked.

"I want to uncover it, Fred," said Leo. "And I need your help. We can reveal everything, and punish the people involved. You're the most direct connection."

"My father has passed. Mother's mind is gone. Who is there to hurt?"

"They were not the only guilty ones," said Leo. "Simonson himself is in that picture, who knows who else—"

"And what will happen to me? My brother, my sisters?" asked Fred. "Do you not think there will be repercussions? That we won't pay for this as well? Are we not complicit?"

"The truth matters," said Leo.

Fred stood up.

"The truth comes at a cost!" said Frederic. "I know more than anyone. Think about the consequence of your actions."

"Fred," said Leo. "Ple—"

"I'll ask that you leave," said Frederic.

"I have nothing else," said Leo. "I need—"

"You should go before I call the police," he said. He handed over the picture, back to Leo. Fred opened the office door and looked away from Leo. Leo left, past Angelica, who stood in the kitchen, washing dishes. She watched Leo as he went.

Leo stepped outside, and the door slammed behind him. He retreated to his car.

He sat in his car, dusk settling in. Frederic wouldn't cooperate, and Leo was stuck. Would any of the other kids help him? He had no idea.

They had careers, families. Accusations, even corroborated, would damage them. It was foolish to think they would just throw their lives away. They'd lose friends and connections. They would lose peace.

Trevor's death rattle echoed through Leo's mind.

They hadn't seen a man die. They didn't realize what he went through to get here.

What options did he have?

Retreat wasn't one. Truth would follow him until he did his duty. He knew it. Frederic was a dead end unless Leo wanted to be arrested.

Barbara. She was alive, riddled with dementia, but still alive. Maybe she could tell him something, or he could find some evidence in that giant old mansion. Her house was being watched, and they'd spot him for sure if he went there. But there were no other options.

A knock on his window startled him. It was Angelica. She stood outside the car, looking inside, harried. He rolled it down.

"Fred is in the bathroom," she said. "I don't have much time. Take this. She'll help."

A post-it note. Angelica pushed it into his palm.

"Why?" asked Leo.

"I've seen the pain they've caused him," she said, and she left him, hurrying back to the house. She disappeared inside.

He unfolded the paper. A name.

Ami Collins.

15

Leo sat in the venom, in the bile. It soaked through his anchor chair. It seeped into his skin.

It was settling into his gut, filling it with poison. The pain, the ache, was getting harder and harder to live with.

Everything had been smooth. Leo let John and Warren take the lead in the pre-production meeting, and encouraged both of their ideas. Next month they would introduce a new segment, where he and John would rapid-fire discuss topics, butting heads.

"The two of you together would be dynamite," said Warren.

Leo nodded and smiled. He wouldn't live to see next *week* at this rate. The poison was eating away inside of him.

Doing this was killing him.

The show ran on autopilot. Leo delivered the segments, transitioned between in-studio news, on location reporting, John's segment, and monologue.

News about the President authorizing new targets for drone strikes, with an increased possibility of civilian casualties, in the name of stopping terrorists. Leo called it a bold, brave idea, and the venom poured inside.

A report about the latest shooting, this time at a broadcast station in Kansas. They had run a piece about a shady local business. The owner had stormed the building, slaying twelve before committing suicide. Leo labeled it a tragedy, but insisted on the rights to own assault weapons, to defend against attacks like this. His stomach burned.

A monologue about the freedom of speech, regarding a march against the President, and how we must be responsible with our freedoms. Exercising them in such a way was dangerous, and should be monitored.

Leo walked to the bathroom, as fast as he could without running. He threw up acid into his sinuses, burning each breath.

He washed his face, spitting up the remainder into the sink. Leo gargled with the tap water. He looked into the mirror, the makeup smudging. He was wrong, wrong every time. Truth wasn't punishing him, not anymore. She was there. He could still feel her, but she was not doing this. She spoke only in truth.

This was his making, his doing. He created it all, this house of venom, and all she did was open his eyes. He recognized his complicity and it was burning him alive from the inside. It was always there, behind the facade he had built to keep him blinded.

He saw the vile now.

He hid in his office, where he could breathe a little bit. It hurt to be here. It stung more every day. It was exponential. Eating him up. He sat at his desk, head in hands, taking deep breaths.

Oh, Truth, please help.

QUIT

A knock at his door and Warren was there.

"Good show today, Leo. Less fire than yesterday, but that's to be expected," said Warren, looking up over his glasses. "You ok?"

"I think I'm fighting off something," said Leo.

"You just can't catch any breaks," said Warren.

"You're not wrong," said Leo, squeezing the bridge of his nose. He wanted Warren to leave so he could go home. It hurt less there. He could prepare the next step, work on the case more. Pay down his ledger more.

"I've been hearing things from the top again," said Warren. "About your behavior off the job."

"What about my behavior?" asked Leo. "I've only been back for two goddamn days. I've quit drinking. What do they want from me?"

"You have to stop," said Warren.

"Stop what?" asked Leo. If they wanted to play this game, Leo could do it as well as anyone. "I've literally done everything asked of me. I took time off. I stopped drinking. I opened up the rest of the show to John, and still—"

"Leo, they see what you're doing," said Warren, taking off his glasses now, speaking lower. "They are watching you, following you."

"What do you know, Warren?" asked Leo.

"I don't know anything, Leo," said Warren. "I keep it that way. I told you before, the less I know, the less trouble I have. They will hurt you, Leo."

Leo looked up then, glanced at Warren, read him. A look of genuine concern on his face.

"I know, Warren," said Leo. "A man is dead already. And I just can't drop it."

Truth will protect him. Truth will protect him.

"Don't," said Warren. "Don't me tell that. Don't tell me anything. If you continue down this path, my hands are tied. Nothing is worth this."

"Truth is," said Leo, down, into his desk. "She's worth it."

"What did you say?" asked Warren.

"The truth is worth it," said Leo. "I said the truth is worth it."

.

Ami Collins. Leo stared at the post-it note.

He pulled up his research on her, what little he could find. She lived just outside of Augusta, Maine. She was a nurse. Unmarried, with a daughter, three years of age. Not much else he could get without paying someone.

Angelica gave him her name, said she would help. Did she have more proof, more pictures?

He had her number. He called, using a burner cell phone. He had bought it at Wal Mart.

She picked up.

"Hello?" she asked. He could hear a child in the background.

"Hi, is this Ami Collins?" he asked.

"I go by Ami Millbury now," she said. "But yes. May I ask who I'm talking to?

"I'm Leo Price. I have a show—" he said.

"I know who you are," she said. "I have a television."

"Well, I'm working on a book about your parents, and I was wondering if I could talk to you about them," he said. "I talked to Frederic recently."

"He'll never give you anything," she said. "He's still too fucked up over it. Can't blame him, but he hasn't worked through it."

"Worked through what?" asked Leo.

"What those fuckers did to us," she said. "Angelica texted me, told me you'd come sniffing. You can drop the charade. I'll help, however I can."

"I want to interview you," he said.

"No time like the present," she said. "Let me put Mary to bed, first. She shouldn't hear it."

"It'd be better in person," he said. "I don't know if someone is listening."

"I don't have any PTO," she said.

"I'll come up there," he said. "I can be there Saturday evening. Does that work?"

It did. She gave him the address.

Truth was there now. He could feel her. He pulled out the photo, held it, and a golden aura washed over him, banishing the pain away. She would heal him and reward him for his duty. He would go to Ami, and he would get evidence. It would lead to more information.

He'd be a real newsman again. And she would fill him with truth.

.

The next couple days of the show were filled with agony. He behaved normally. It was business as usual. Leo was the perfect actor, even as the garbage he spewed piled up around him. John was excited and genial. Leo could have almost described him as *nice*. He offered to take Leo out for a night on the town over the weekend, but Leo declined.

Warren was the same as ever, with no more cryptic warnings. The show went well, so well Leo was on the verge of tears by Thursday. He took every over the counter pain medication he could find. They did nothing. And he wouldn't touch the opioids. He'd end up in the same boat as with the booze.

Truth led him here, and he would continue to follow her. She would protect him.

He got through the week. No show on Friday. He woke up early that day, the sky still dark, and packed.

A few days worth of clothes. His laptop and tablet. And fishing gear, his box and tackle, and his rod. It would serve as cover. Maine had good fishing, and the season wasn't over yet.

He drove. It was long.

The last time he fished was years ago now. How did he let it get away from him? He had loved it. It was how he bonded with Alex. Even with all the arguments and the strife between them, they always had fishing.

He had worried the first time he had brought Alex. He was still a kid, eleven, and Leo had feared he would lack the patience required. But he was a natural and settled right into the routine. The simple rhythm of casting and reeling in came naturally to Alex. Even at his age, he had the focus to catch one when it finally bit. Alex was so happy when he reeled it in, glowing up at Leo.

The peace and quiet, moments with Alex. It was great.

He had the time then. He hadn't started The Truth yet.

Leo remembered their last outing. Alex came home from school, and they went fishing. Just like the good old days. Alex drove, and Leo drank more than he should. He didn't need to drive. Who cares if he hit the bottle a little too much?

He had gotten sloppy and Alex cut the day short. Leo couldn't remember it exactly, but he had insisted that he was fine, and they could continue. Alex brought him back to his house and left him there, after a brief goodbye.

How did he not realize it? He was a fucking mess then. Did Alex see him the same, even now?

Truth had set him right. She had scorched out the bad in him. She had made him great again, like the man he once was. He would be a journalist again, who broke stories, who raised his kids right, who loved his wife and found time for her. Truth did it all. He would repay her for her kindness.

The drive was long, and the sun rose. Two hours in, panic struck him. He pulled over. His tires screeched as he jerked the car to the side of the interstate. He rummaged through his pockets, and his bag. No, no he had left it. He hit the steering wheel with a fist, pounding on it, furious at himself.

Two hours out. He could go on without it. He had pictures of it. That was good enough, surely. He didn't need to go back. It was a waste of time. Four hours gone, his whole schedule ruined. He didn't need to go back.

He pulled back onto the interstate and drove, his stomach roiling with anxiety, sweat starting to pour down his back. He drove for ten minutes more, and then pulled through a utility U-Turn. He turned around. Leo needed the printout.

He drove home. The sun was well up by the time he returned.

Leo walked in, straight not to his safe, but to his bed. He pulled off the sheets, down to the bare mattress. He found the small slice he made in the soft cotton and slipped his hand inside, fishing until he located the battered piece of paper. Leo unfolded it, looked at it. Just to make sure. It was his.

He folded it, slid it into a front pocket. Back to the car. Back on the road.

He drove. It was long.

He arrived at the motel around seven. He ordered a pizza and ate it while going over his research, again and again, scouring for any clue. His eyes closed, the day of driving taking its toll.

He slept, the picture under his pillow.

16

Leo went fishing. It was beautiful. He was in Fairfield, Maine, north of Augusta. He dropped his gear on the coast, and waded out into the cool water, just south of the Shawmut Dam.

The sun was still down, and he let the sound of the river push his worries away.

And then Jeremy Hammond showed up, an hour after sunrise.

He heard Jeremy approach from behind, a massive satchel of stuff that he had brought with him, loaded onto his broad shoulders.

A canopy, opened, ten by ten.

A chair, a stove, a cooler.

Plus all of his fishing gear.

That was all fine, even though he made enough noise to wake the dead setting it all up, stomping around, driving the canopy stakes into the ground with a mallet like an obese circus strongman. It was public land. Leo stood out in the shallows, casting, reeling, ignoring the commotion from the shore. He wasn't getting any bites, but the fishing wasn't about catching fish.

And then Jeremy began playing radio country over a Bluetooth speaker. The sound echoed over the water.

Leo looked back, as Jeremy cooked hamburgers on his camp stove, whistling to the music wafting over to Leo.

He waited. Maybe Jeremy would see him standing there, realize that he was disrupting someone else's peace, and he would turn off the radio. The minutes ticked by, with Leo knee deep in the water, waiting, waiting. He looked back again, finally. Jeremy saw him, lifted a beer toward him, smiling.

He sighed. A few hours of calm before facing Ami Collins was all he wanted.

He walked over to Jeremy.

"Excuse me," said Leo. "Would you mind switching off your music, or at least turning it down? I came out here to enjoy the quiet, and—"

"Holy shit!" said Jeremy, standing up, spilling his beer all over himself, dwarfing Leo. "You're Leo Price!"

"I—"

"You're Leo Price," said Jeremy. "Jeremy Hammond. Huge fan. Huuuuuge fan. I can't believe it. I can't believe you're here." Jeremy extended a big hand, a lopsided smile on his face. Leo shook it.

"Nice to meet a supporter," said Leo. "Would you mind

turning off your music?"

"Anything for you, Mr. Price," said Jeremy, pushing a button on the speaker, silencing it. "You have no idea."

He gave Leo an idea. Jeremy was a huge man, six foot six, and nearly four hundred pounds. It wasn't a guess on Leo's part, because Jeremy told Leo it all. He was happy to share everything about himself with Leo because he was Leo's biggest fan. He watched every episode of The Truth, moderated a The Truth Facebook page, and frequented his subreddit, which Leo himself almost never visited. Jeremy described his fandom, detailing his love of the show and of Leo himself. Finally, he talked about his own Youtube channel, patterned after The Truth.

Leo couldn't go anywhere without seeing evidence of the damage done. It was following him.

The man went on and on, showing Leo a video from his Youtube channel, filmed in his garage. In the video, Jeremy shouted about the exhaust on his new car. He yelled about "the snowflakes pussifying his car just like they were pussifying America." The recording washed over Leo.

"Jeremy," said Leo, finally interrupting him. Jeremy paid rapt attention to him. "I'll be here until early afternoon. I wanted a peaceful day, where I could relax, and stare at the water, and fish. If you ensure I get that, I will film a short video with you for your channel, before I leave. Do we have a deal?"

"Oh man," said Jeremy. "Absolutely, Mr. Price. I'll be as quiet as a fart in church." He mimed zipping up his lips and throwing it in the river.

Leo walked out into the river. He cast, reeled. The occasional noise would spring up from behind him, but Jeremy was a man of his word and kept his great bulk silent.

The hours passed, and Leo felt good again. The same aura from before settled on him as the water flowed by his ankles. Truth was with him again. He could feel her. She was in his bones, and the water carried away the poison, little by little. He was on a righteous mission again, and it satisfied her. He knew it.

It hit early afternoon and he packed up his few things. A man of his word, he filmed a short promo video for Jeremy's Youtube channel. It hurt him to do it. But Leo only had himself to blame.

·

Ami's apartment was small, tucked into the back of a large cookie cutter building in Augusta. The sun was setting as Leo knocked on her door. She answered quietly, her finger to her mouth in a shhing motion, extending the other to shake his hand. She smiled gently.

She was a tiny woman, five foot tall, thin. Her hair was long and dreadlocked.

"I just got Mary to sleep," she said, her voice low. "We can talk in the kitchen."

Leo nodded and followed her into the room, down the short entrance hallway.

She pulled a chair out for him at the small dinette set.

"Would you like some coffee?" she asked.

"That'd be great, actually," he said. She made some, her back to him, and then joined him.

"You came a long way to talk to me," she said. "It lends to your credibility."

"I understand if you don't trust me," he said.

"I have faith in you, Mr. Price," she said, cutting him off.

"I've read your work, before your program. And this story is not one for your typical audience. You want to reveal the Collins? And the others?"

"Yes," he said. "All of them. The truth."

"Where do we begin?" she asked.

"Let me show you this first," he said, pulling out the worn picture and handing it to her.

She opened and examined it. The raw emotion, the vulnerability wasn't there like it was with Frederic. She was reading the phone book.

"That stupid son of a bitch," she said. "That giant digital camera. Probably cost a couple of thousand dollars, back then. And Simonson, right there. Bunch of idiots."

"Do you remember him?" asked Leo.

"No," she said, handing the picture back to him. "There were so many of them, and I was young. They were just white men, friends of Charlie."

"Did anyone besides Charlie…" asked Leo. He looked at her, not knowing how to ask.

"Rape me?" she asked. "It's ok, Mr. Price. You won't hurt my feelings. Yes, once in a while. Charlie would hand me off, or one of my sisters, to different men."

"When did it start?" he asked.

"Right away," she said. "I was thirteen when I was adopted. When I first arrived, I didn't know how to feel. Lucky, I guess. The orphanage back home was poor, and there was nothing that set me apart from the rest of the children. I have no idea why the Collins picked me. Random chance, maybe. I don't know. Have you been to their house, Mr. Price?"

"Yes," he said. "Once or twice. I think we met, when you

were still a child."

"Do you remember what you thought of it?" she asked.

"Big," he said. "Clean. Ornate."

"Those are good words for it," she said. "It felt impossible, the first time there. Why was I so lucky, to be in this impossible house, pulled away from poverty? I don't remember everything, but I distinctly recall a gnawing feeling in my gut, like it was too good to be true, that they would pull me away, throw me back into a plane, and I would be back at the orphanage. Poor again. Hungry."

"But everything was real. I met my siblings. Met Charlie and Barbara. Met the 'help'. The servants! *I* would have servants. The anxiety was gone by the time I laid down to sleep in my own bedroom. There was no catch, no bait and switch. I *was* just that lucky. I was wrong."

"Was it the first night?" he asked.

"Charlie woke me up, in the middle of the night," she said. "And pulled me away, to a different room. Not his bedroom, a room I didn't see when I was shown the house. And he raped me. The first time of many."

"Did you know what was happening?"

"I was a child, but I wasn't stupid. The nuns taught me about men, about what they want. And I realized that as soon as he dragged me out of bed. I knew what was going on, and I realized this was the cost."

"Why didn't you say anything?" he asked. "Any of you?"

"Barbara," she said. "She kept us quiet. If she heard us talking about it with our siblings, she'd beat, torture, and imprison us. She told us, again and again—that we were black, we were African, no one would trust us, and they would send us back, and we would starve in the streets.

Over, and over."

"And you believed her," he said.

"I did, because she was right, Mr. Price," she said. "No one would believe us. You remember those parties. Our black faces in a sea of white. Everywhere we went, it was the same. People did not talk to us, they talked *at* us. The charity covered for everything. No one would believe us."

"And it continued until you left?"

"Until I fled for college," she said. "Five years. I was lucky, only had five years in hell before I got out of there. The others, they were younger. It was worse for them."

"All of you were abused?" he said.

"Yes," she said, unequivocally. "Each in different ways, but all hurt. The girls were all raped, all by Charlie, some by other men, passed around his inner circle, used as a reward, or a test of loyalty. The boys, Fred and Daniel, both were raped by Barbara, and by a few men, I think. They never admitted it, but it seemed likely."

"How many people know about this?" asked Leo. "Who knew what was going on?"

"Hundreds," she said. "At least. The in-group changed over time, and they came and went until we all were gone, and Charlie died."

"And no one said anything," he said. "No leaks."

"Of the many who were present or took part, and then all who heard something, or told someone who whispered it to someone else, you are the only one to come to me. Why would they reveal truth? They would be complicit. What would they gain from revealing the horror?"

Complicit. The same word Fred used.

"Truth is its own reward," said Leo.

"I imagine their definition differs from yours, Mr. Price," she said.

They talked for hours. Ami gave all the detail she could remember, confirmed what she knew or suspected. Leo listened, took notes, and recorded it all. He could feel Truth floating around him, in him. She approved, he could tell. The poison was being pulled out of him. She was doing it, he knew.

"Do you have any direct evidence?" he asked.

"Other than my word?" she asked. "No. It 'd surprise me if any of us did. We had no possessions. Barbara made sure. Anything that could prove any wrongdoing was taken from us. After a while, we stopped trying. It wasn't worth the extra pain."

"Than this picture is all we have," he said. "Plus your account, and any of your siblings that will help."

"It won't be enough," she said. "But there's evidence, I'm almost sure of it."

"Where?" asked Leo.

"With Barbara, in that house," she said. "Charlie's office is still there. I was there, for the funeral, and everything was still in that room, untouched. She has lost her mind. *If* you can get in. It shouldn't be that hard."

"You haven't called them your parents one time," he said. "Frederic called them mother and father."

"He still has their name," she said. "I got rid of it as soon as I could."

"Even after divorce?" he asked.

"It didn't work out. But my ex's name is worth more than theirs," she said. "Give Fred some time. He'll come around. Most of them will, once they understand what you're trying to do."

It was late by the time he was done. He would return to the motel, and then drive back to DC tomorrow.

"Can I ask you one more question before I go?"

"Only if I can ask you one first," said Ami.

"Shoot," he said.

"Why are you doing this?" she asked. "And don't tell me because of old fashioned journalistic integrity. What happened to you?"

Leo stopped.

"I've lied too much," he said. "By several measures over. I need to work it back, in the other direction. I don't think I'll be the host of my show much longer."

Ami nodded, understanding. "You had a question?"

"Do you think this is worth it?" he asked. "Unearthing all this pain?"

She smiled a joyless smile.

"Of course," said Ami. "They should be smothered with it."

17

The motel was empty and quiet. Leo planned his next move, and then Truth was there with him.

Her presence around and in him was growing. He could feel it, down in his bones, in everything he did. Leo had felt her as he left his house, as he drove the long drive to Maine, and even as he fished with Jeremy Hammond lurking behind him on the shore. Truth lingered as he talked to Ami and she was still here, in the motel. He had felt her the whole time.

When she had first appeared she was cold. When she had screamed her truth at him, it had filled him with that same cold. And as he resisted, she got colder. Truth had absorbed all the warmth from him. She had blistered him with her scream. She had tormented him.

But then he let her in, and she was sharing her spirit with him.

He remembered her appearance in his home. Towering, decrepit, bloodless, massive eyes and mouth, body stretched, hair floating around them both, imprisoning him.

She had haunted him, followed him, to his house, to his job, to the beach. But now he understood.

She was here again, and she showed him she had more than one form.

Leo sat in bed, his laptop open in his lap. He put his notes from Ami's interview into the massive document and organized the evidence. Then he felt her approach. The warmth in his chest expanded and grew, ambrosia filling him from within.

And she was there, floating above him, unrestrained. Her form before was skeletal, drained white hide stretched over bone. No more. The once empty figure was full, soft, and warm, her skin glowing like sunlight. She was nude, not terrifying, but welcoming. No longer asymmetrical or inhuman. Her face, once monstrous eyes and mouth, was human and suffused with love. Her hair flowed around her again, hovering with her, but not a prison. Now they were robes. They were home.

She did not smile, for she did know how, but she knew peace, and she showed it to Leo.

It was night, and Leo was sitting in his car, in a parking garage.

A light appeared, in the darkness from Leo's left. It flashed, once, twice, three times. His source was here. He got out, the surroundings quiet.

"You made it," said Leo.

"It took some doing," said the man, from the shadows.

"Please, don't come any closer."

"I can't get your name?" asked Leo. "See your face?"

"I'm sorry," he said. "It's too dangerous. It's safer if you don't know."

"Do you have the information?" he asked. "About the lobbyists?"

"I do," he said. A manila envelope sailed out of the darkness and skidded to a stop at Leo's feet. He ripped it open, flipping through the pages.

"It's in there, if you dig," he said. "I can't tell you anything more than that. It would reveal me, and I can't have that happen. Not yet."

He was a journalist now, a true reporter, last of a dying breed. His story about the Collins broke everything open, and with it, he had launched his own news outlet. Every report he wrote got more attention than ever before. Every piece worked at erasing his past at The Truth. He spoke honestly about his time there, and people respected him for his change of heart, for his search for redemption through truth.

He was with Diana at the beach house.

He was making dinner. Grilled chicken with a simple pasta, dressed with olive oil and pesto. A Caesar salad on the side for both of them. It was almost ready when she came home. She drove into the city to meet with her publisher and her agent, to work out a new contract.

She hugged him. Embraced him, squeezed him hard, and kissed him on the lips, soft.

"How'd it go?" he asked.

"It went well," she said. "Five more books. Bigger deal than before."

"You deserve every penny," he said. "Where would they be without you?"

"They'd have five fewer books," she said. "It smells great in here. What are we having?"

"Grilled chicken and pasta," he said. "Very fancy."

"I wouldn't have married you if I wanted fancy," she said. "I'm going to shower, and I'll be right down."

She showered, and they ate dinner, with casual conversation, nothing that exciting. But they were together, and happy in each other's company. Leo recognized this man, the one he used to be, before the show, before he became Leo Price.

They were all together again.

Alex and Jen were visiting, and they were all out at dinner. Jen brought her girlfriend Liz for the first time. Alex, his wife Patricia, and little William were there as well.

"This place is great," said Alex.

"Your mother picked it," she said. "She has an eye for good restaurants. It has something for everyone."

"Jen tells us you're a barista, Liz," said Diana.

"Yeah, for now," she said. "It's just to pay the bills."

"No shame in that," said Leo.

"You want to share a dessert, dad?" asked Jen. They shared when she was a kid. They were the sweet tooths.

"I think I could manage that," he said, teasing at his belt, smiling.

She ordered a brownie with ice cream, and Leo surveyed the table. Everyone was chatting and happy. All together, all peaceful. They would go their separate ways soon, return to the new lives they were building for themselves.

And he was back in the motel, with Truth floating above

him, an angel.

What was she showing him? What could have been? Or what still could be? Would this be his reward for following her? A new career? A family rebuilt, reassembled?

She could do all of that, and more. Truth would show him the way. He had looked into her eyes. Her wide gleaming eyes, open, innocent and full of wonder, told him it was true. Leo would embark on her mission, and find all he missed when he started the show.

All the fear and the rage, all the horror she had shown him before was wiped away. She showed him love, and warmth, and that was all he wanted, all he needed now. She floated above him and everything bad was gone. Only the honesty of devotion remained.

And then his phone rang, and Truth vanished.

He looked at it, not recognizing the number, answering anyway.

"Hello," he said.

"Hello, Leo," said the voice, a familiar one, one he heard before. The cleaner. The murderer. The face he couldn't remember who strangled Trevor to death in a swamp. "We speak again."

"Fuck you, killer," said Leo, the anger, the injustice right there.

"Oh please," said the voice. "You can muster that outrage on a dime, can't you?"

"What do you want?" asked Leo.

"Do you remember what I told you before, when we spoke?" asked the cleaner.

"Why should I listen to you?" asked Leo.

"I told you to get rid of that picture. I said to forget about it, about Trevor, about this whole mess, and you would have no problems. I told you all that as a courtesy."

"Fuck your courtesy," said Leo.

"I do have my limits, Leo," said the voice. "And you're testing them. That was a favor because of who you are. Leo Price. Famous TV host, with connections to powerful individuals. And I in*structed* you to get rid of that picture. But you haven't, have you? You've gone around, talked to more people, showed it around, endangered more lives, made my life harder."

They still followed him. He thought driving all this way would throw them off the scent. He used burner phones, new email addresses. There was no escaping them.

"Do you think you can just do whatever you want? That you're invincible?" asked the voice. "It doesn't matter how careful you are, you are vulnerable. Everything can and will be taken from you."

"I'm following the truth," said Leo.

The killer laughed. Loud, uproarious laughter. Honest laughter.

"Woo boy," he said. "I've met some true psychos in my day, but you take the cake, Leo. That is truly funny, coming from you."

"I'm not afraid of you," said Leo. He was filled with Truth, and nothing could stop him.

"You're not afraid?" said the voice. "What about Alex? Or Jennifer? Or Diana? They can disappear just like your source, never to be heard from again."

"Touch them and I'll—"

"Do what, Leo?" asked the voice. "This is your final warning. Drop it, now, and you will never hear from me again. You'll have your show, your life. This will all be a bad dream."

"How can you do this?" asked Leo. "Where's your conscience?"

"Leo, I would love to talk more, but I'm not getting paid for your sanctimony," said the voice.

"The truth matters," said Leo.

The voice laughed again and hung up.

The killer's words were still on Leo's mind as he drove home the next day. Did Leo believe him? Would the killer hurt his children, go after Diana? He didn't think so. Empty threats. Leo was the one they pursued, and they wouldn't do a thing, not while he was on the air.

Truth was with him and she reassured him. He must continue his pursuit, to punish those who buried the truth. She would help him. She would protect him. By the time he got home on Sunday, the sun was fading, and he should have been tired after a long drive.

He felt invigorated instead. Truth filled him with purity of purpose, with righteousness. He finished his planning and worked out the rest of the investigation. Leo would get into the Collins' house and find the evidence he needed to demonstrate his case.

He would prove the killer wrong, just like everyone else.

18

Leo knew they would fire him before he even got to work. He went in anyway.

Truth woke him up that Monday morning. A gentle stirring, better than any alarm clock, always effective. She roused him, and something was different. Leo knew it like he knew his birthday. There was no vision, no message from her. Only bare knowledge. He knew that when he went in for work, he'd be coming back home, no matter what he did.

Warren was waiting for him in his office.

Leo smiled at him. He would not make this easy. "Morning, Warren. Something I can help you with?"

"You're done, Leo," said Warren.

"Done?" asked Leo. "Done with what? Thought we had three more days of the report from Wisconsin about that pesticide."

"You're fired, Leo," said Warren. "You are no longer the host of The Truth."

"That a fact?" asked Leo, putting his bag down on the couch, facing Warren.

"It's a fact," said Warren.

"Why?" asked Leo.

"Are we really going to do this—"

"Why, Warren?" asked Leo. "Tell me why. I want to hear you say it."

"The network isn't happy with your performance lately," said Warren. "They see John as a strong candidate to lead the show moving forward and whom carries none of your baggage."

"Bullshit," said Leo, raising his voice. "Bullshit, Warren. Don't you fucking lie, not after all this time. Ratings are higher than ever, and despite what John may think, I am still the face of The Truth. So don't you dare lie. You're better than that."

Warren only stared daggers at him.

"Say it, Warren," said Leo. "I want the truth."

Warren stared, and inhaled, deep.

"I warned you," said Warren. "I warned you, multiple times."

"Warned me?" asked Leo. "Warned me about what?"

"Damn you," said Warren. "I warned you to keep your goddamn head down, to keep your nose out of business it doesn't belong in, and you couldn't goddamn listen. You got some bug up your ass, and you had to throw it all away chasing after some story, to relieve your conscience or chase the glory days—"

"Story of the century," said Leo. "Story of the goddamn century, and you want to put your head in the sand and ignore it. What happened to you?"

Warren only stared.

"Do you know that I was afraid before I met you the first time?" asked Leo. "I was a grown man, an accomplished journalist, and I was literally shaking. I was anxious because of who you were, of what you had done, of who you had worked with."

Leo got closer to him.

"You had such a reputation, and look at you now. Kowtowing to those bastards, because you're afraid," said Leo. "Scared of exposing your masters."

"You shut your fucking mouth," said Warren.

"Or what? You'll fire me?" asked Leo. "You'll hit me? I'm not frightened of you anymore, Warren. And no one else is either. Anything to say?"

Warren smiled, finally.

"You," he said. "You say this. Leo Price, host of The Truth. Voice and face of the show. Famous worldwide. I made you who you are. I did it. And you would throw it all away. Burn it all down."

"It's toxic, Warren," said Leo. "We are broadcasting poison and venom every single fucking day and they eat it up with a spoon, and I'm supposed to just keep to business as usual?"

"Who the fuck cares?" asked Warren. "Who are you? A hero, now? After years of this? I've worked in television for decades, and guess what, the only difference between this show and legitimate news was the pay, in that here, I get paid what I'm worth. The people out there don't know the difference, and they honestly don't care."

"We are feeding them poison!"

"It is what they deserve," said Warren, finally. "They want it. I'm sorry it's the way the world is, Leo. I really am. But we are only filling a need. If it wasn't us, it'd be somebody else. Hell, it already is someone else. There are a dozen men like you, and more every day, and they all are getting paid because there's so *much* demand. Your severance package is on your desk. After I leave, security will give you an hour to clear out your office."

Warren left without a glance backward. Leo wanted to shout after him, to scream at the person he once considered his mentor. But there was no going back. Truth had changed him, and Warren didn't know her. Didn't realize what she could do to a man. Warren hadn't seen what Leo had.

He packed his things. There wasn't much, after seven years. No awards. A few keepsakes. Framed photos of Alex and Jen. He went through his desk, through the papers that amassed over the years inside.

The breakdown and run-through of the first episode. The main story was about fist bumping. He remembered thinking how stupid it was at the time, but the ratings were through the roof. Warren pushed it through. He had told Leo to trust him.

Or was it Leo that pushed it through?

His memory was foggy, and the thin sheaf of papers did nothing to clear it out. More and more plans for stories. Most of them never saw the light of day. They chased what was hot, and it didn't leave time for his ideas. They went into the desk.

Why did he keep all this crap? Stacks of paper, some

filed, some thrown into a pile in the lowest drawer. None of it worthwhile. All of it soaked with lies and venom. He could feel it. Just touching it was soaking into his skin. He would throw up if he didn't drop them. He threw them all back in his desk. He needed none of it. They could throw it all away.

Leo grabbed the pictures and left everything else. It was all tinged with death and worth nothing.

Security escorted him out, his framed pictures in his briefcase. He kept his head up, even as they whispered as he passed, the two brutes flanking him, making sure he did nothing rash on his way out.

He drove home, and his publicist called. Mary Walters. She was good at her job.

"Leo," she said. "What the hell is going on?"

"They fired me, Mary," he said. "They're putting John in my place."

"They can't do that," she said. "I'll start the spin."

"Don't," he said.

"What? We need to do something. We can't let the network control the discussion," she said.

"I don't want to fight it," he said. "I don't have the energy for it."

"But it's everything," she said. "It's your show."

"Release a statement, to everyone," he said. "Say we came to a mutual understanding to end my contract, and that I will pursue independent work."

"Is that true?" she asked. "You don't tell me these things? I'm like a mushroom over here."

"I can't tell you everything," he said. "But I'm working on something big, and when it breaks, it'll open up business.

I'll go solo, start my own outlet online."

"You're signing the check," she said. "Anything else you want me to add?"

"Yes," he said. "I want it to say that from now on, I'll be pursuing the truth."

"Ooookay," she said. "I'll type it up and send it out. Do you want press?"

"Not yet," he said. "After."

"And that's it?" she asked. "Radio silence?"

"For now," he said. "Trust me."

"I'll get to work."

Leo was alone again in his home.

No, not alone. Truth was there. He could feel her. She never left him, not anymore.

It was a weight off his shoulders. Even in Maine, knee-deep in river water, Leo felt the poison. It found its way to him. The toxins worked their way from the studio, from that bastard chair. Firing him did him a favor.

Leo was lighter than air. He felt better than he had in years. His breath and thoughts came easily. His mind was clear, and clarity of purpose was what he needed right now. To unearth the truth, he'd have to be sharp.

Truth would help h—

He was in the swamp again.

Not again, no, please. He couldn't watch Trevor die again. He couldn't bear to see her as she had been, see her skeletal frame, her wide eyes, hear her scream—

He was behind them, behind them again as the killer marched Trevor out into the mud, out of the killer's car, out to the marshland where he would strangle him to death, and leave his body to rot. His wife would never know, his wife would never know never know—

"Did you think that would work?" asked the killer, Trevor on a noose leash. "Did you really think that would work on me? I've seen everything, every trick in the book. I wanted to make it easy, but you're trying my patience."

He was pulled along, just like before. He couldn't look away. Why was Truth showing him this? He did what she said, he felt her warmth—

There was no response from Trevor. The noose was too tight around his neck, and he didn't have enough breath to talk. Every effort was met with a tug from the killer. He didn't want a discussion. He wanted a monologue.

"It's a shame," he said. "It didn't have to come to this."

There was a small mercy for Leo. Truth wasn't there, wasn't staring at him from the shadows.

They stopped, at the edge of the water. He'd have to watch again, have to see Trevor slowly suffocate and die, with no way to help, no means to stop the killer. Leo couldn't even look at the killer's face, still couldn't remember it from the last time, and Truth wasn't showing it to him now.

"Sorry, buddy," he said. "Time to die."

And then he was back.

Leo gasped, his heart pounding. What was going on? He felt for Truth, and she was there, no fear or anger he could sense. He caught his breath, drank some water.

Was it punishment? He did everything for her, all for her. He wouldn't disappoint her, not again.

It was motivation, incentive. Must be. A reminder of what *they* did already, and why he must succeed.

He had to move quickly. The firing, the vision. It was to push him to action. He had Ami's interview, but he needed hard evidence. None of the kids would have it. They could corroborate, but he lacked the proof. And Ami said it was still in the Collins' house, hidden behind servants and Barbara's senility.

He could get in, he would figure o—

He couldn't breathe

The killer was behind him. Trevor pulled at the noose, tightening, tightening, the thick rope cutting off his air. Leo watched it happen, but he couldn't breathe.

"Stop your struggling," said the killer, straining, his chest heaving. "I've done this enough times. There's no way out. This is the end."

Leo wanted to do something, needed to grab the killer from behind, knock him to the ground, not suffocate him, but beat him, hit him, pound him until his face was broken and bloody, and then, when there was nothing left of him to beat, he'd drown him in the muck, and make sure he knew that no one would ever find him, and nobody would care that he was gone.

But he couldn't do a thing. He was trapped as an observer, and he questioned again why Truth was giving him this vision. Why was she showing him Trevor again?

He coughed and he was back at his computer again. His breath came in short gasps. He shook his head, his heart pounding through his chest.

"Don't worry," he said, to Truth, who he knew was there. "I'm working, working for you. Working to discover the evidence. That's all we need."

Leo went back into his notes and looked at the long list of Collins children. They were spread through the country and the world. He would talk to all of them and find out who would help. Together they would unearth the truth.

But he needed the hard proof to back it up, to give the public the facts they needed to see. And it was only in one place.

Did they even know? Barbara wasn't a threat, not to anyone. From all reports, she barely remembered her own name. Or thought it was thirty years ago.

He bet it was still there, buried on a hard drive, or in a forgotten drawer or shelf. He was certain of it. He could feel Truth's guidance. She was pushing him toward Barbara because everything they needed was there.

He would find a way in and get the information he needed to uncover the truth.

19

Leo smiled as he knocked on the door. It was wide and genuine because it would need to be wide and genuine.

A young man answered, in his early twenties. He was clean cut and wore a cardigan over a collared shirt. Leo smiled even wider. This kid was his primary obstacle to Barbara Collins.

"Hi," said Leo. "May I speak to Barbara Collins?"

"Do you have an appointment?" he asked. "She's sleeping at the moment."

"What's your name?" asked Leo, extending his hand for a handshake.

"I'm Colin," he said, the door still partly closed. He reached around the edge and grabbed it, a half shake.

"Leo Price," he said. "Host of The Truth."

"On television?" asked Colin. "I'm sorry, I don't watch any TV."

"You've never seen the show?" asked Leo.

"Sorry, no," he said. "I gather you don't have an appointment."

"I tried to reach out for one, but I ran into a bunch of dead ends. Thought it'd be much easier to just come down here and say hello in person. I was an acquaintance of Ms. Collins years ago, and I was hoping I could talk to her again."

"I'm sorry, Mr.—Price, did you say," he said. "You probably are aware that Barbara is not always there, you know, mentally, and today hasn't been great so far. Why do you want to speak to her again?"

He was stonewalling Leo. This wouldn't do. Leo found his persona.

"The show is quite popular, and I'm taking a break to research a project all about the Collins, both Barbara and Charlie. Barbara is rather famous for her parties and her charity work, and I wanted to paint it in the best light, and I thought, what a better place than straight from the source. I actually attended a few of their banquets, back in the good old days."

"I—"

"And I had gotten some conflicting reports about her charity and those parties. Seems a few people are trying to call into the question the authenticity of their philanthropy, calling it a sham, retroactively. Now I understand that Barbara may not be completely herself, but I still think it's worth a shot to let the woman defend herself."

"I don't think—" said Colin, the door opening wider. There we go.

"Part of the reason I'm working on this project is that I do not want the legacy of the Collins to be soiled. They did so much good for the country, both through politics and through philanthropy, and I'd hate for the rabble-rousers to get a hold of their name and impugn it in front of the world, with neither of them available to defend themselves. I knew Barbara well enough. Maybe some time with her will bring out the old her."

He smiled again, big and genuine. Leo could summon any expression at will. Enough time performing, anyone could.

Colin looked unsure. Couldn't be older than twenty-five, a caretaker for an eighty-five-year-old woman. The kid was waffling. He kept up the big smile. Colin creaked the door open. *Yes.*

"I suppose it can't hurt," he said. "It might be good for her, seeing a familiar face. Come in."

Leo stepped in, and the memories of his last time here came trickling back in, bit by bit. The house was big, three stories, not a stretch to call it a mansion. The entrance opened up into a huge open area, bordered by a bar and a grand piano. French doors looked out onto a massive stone patio with a small pool at the edge. Entertaining had been its primary function, but now was just nursing care for its one remaining inhabitant.

"I'll take you to her sitting room," he said. "You can wait there while I get her."

"You mentioned a familiar face," he said, as they walked up to a set of stairs. "Does she get any visitors?"

"Not often," he said. "I've been here for two years, and including you, it's single digits."

"Her children don't come to visit?" Leo asked.

"No, it's a real shame," said Colin, showing Leo to a smaller room, with four armchairs positioned around a small glass table. Shelves lined every wall, filled with pictures, knick-knacks, and books. "After all that Barbara and Charlie did for them, and they never visit. I'll be back with her. I appreciate your patience. It may take a little while."

Colin disappeared down the hallway, leaving Leo alone in the room. He could have bolted, looked around the whole house, but it wouldn't benefit him in the long term. He had to talk to Barbara. He needed to look her in the eyes.

He would need her help to find the evidence against her.

There were dozens of pictures, and Leo spent his time waiting looking at them. The Collins with every president. With other politicians. With dozens of local celebrities, photo ops at different charity events. The same smiles in each picture plastered on Barbara and Charlie. The same practiced smile that Leo exercised to get inside.

Above all else, there were pictures with the children. All were carefully posed and constructed. They were well dressed, always smiling, ever aware of the camera. They weren't as skilled as Barbara or Charlie. He saw the unease around their eyes. He saw Fred and Ami, out for a trip to a baseball game. Or a zoo, or a dozen of other local landmarks. Their mouths were wide, teeth showing, lips upturned. But they weren't smiling.

"Do you like our pictures, Mr. Price?" asked a voice from behind him. He turned to see the frail figure of Barbara Collins, her thin, shaking hand holding onto Colin's as they entered the room.

The last image he saw of her was in that picture, the

printout still folded in his pocket, weathered and worn now. Twenty years younger, Barbara was clutching onto the last vestiges of middle age, raping a boy fifty years her junior. That illusion was gone, no fade-out, no subtle shift. She was on death's door, a fragile skeleton of a person, her remaining hair white, her spine bent by age. Her absent smile revealed missing teeth. Her cloudy eyes peered at him.

Leo's grin was back, even as he looked at what was left of the woman who abused and raped her children.

"Ms. Collins," he said, extending a hand to her. She reached out her own, and he held it. He felt her fragile hand, like the body of a hummingbird. Weightless, with empty bones.

Break her

Truth was there. The golden aura hardened as they approached the Collins house, and he felt her burning inside of him. The wraith that once haunted him approached. Now that they were in the same room as the monster, it was stronger still, simmering rage boiling over. He must control Truth or she would kill Barbara here and now.

Snap her in half break her bones

Colin led her to a seat and lowered her into it. He set her down like carry-on luggage, her small frame eclipsed by the plush antique chair.

"Some tea, Colin," she said, her voice raspy newspaper.

"Yes, ma'am," he said, walking at a brisk pace out of the room, leaving them alone.

Now now now now now break her PUNISH her

"Colin says you're writing about me and Charlie," she said. "Nothing bad I hope."

Leo looked into her foggy eyes. How much of her was in

there right now, and how much was a patched tire, held together by artifice and a facade of memories? Was the woman that beat her daughters and raped her sons in there? Was it better if she was gone altogether, time erasing her, neuron by neuron?

"Oh yes," he said. "I'm working on a book about both of you. I was hoping I could receive your input."

"I'll do what I can to help," she said. "But my memory isn't what it used to be."

Now

"May I ask a few questions?" he asked. "To get started?"

"Go ahead, go ahead," she said. "I'm not getting any younger."

"I'm writing a whole chapter on your charity work in Africa, and how it lead to you adopting your children," he said. "How did that all get started?"

"I don't remember exactly what happened," she said. "I was reading up on some tragedy there. There was always some civil war or coup d'etat going on, and there was a feature story on the orphans left over from these battles. And they'd be left with no family, no nothing, and it seemed so terrifically sad. I told Charlie, I told him we should try and do something about it."

"And you went to Africa," said Leo. "In 1984. To the Congo."

"Yes," she said. "I had never been, and it was an eye-opening experience. The children lived in misery, after having already lost so much. We started the foundation as soon as I got back home."

Wrong

"We can start a charity helping kids in Africa," said Barbara.

"They're begging for help, and they'll never question your motivations again."

"Africa?" asked Charlie. "Why Africa?"

"Because it's the worst place, Charlie," she said. "There's plenty of places we could help, but Africa is the worst. They will love us forever."

Truth was inside.

"There were no ulterior motives?" he asked, trying his best to keep a neutral voice, and failing.

"Ulterior motives?" she asked, her head craning higher.

"A few of Charlie's more brazen opponents would whisper from time to time that it was all optics," he said, leaning hard into every word.

"So awful," she said. "Ugly words for ugly people. We helped how many children, over the years? And they tried to sully it. Disgusting."

Truth burned inside.

"And this led you to adopting?" he asked.

"We were getting older," she said. "And I couldn't have children. And after meeting the kids over there, it seemed like the perfect solution."

"I want to adopt," he said. "Children from the foundation."

"Are you sure?" she asked.

"They will be perfect," he said. "They'll be ours, and no one will dare question us."

Charlie caressed Barbara's neck, with soft fingers.

Leo blinked, Truth intruding again. Two predators, both of them. They knew what they did, right from the start. Leo looked at the woman in front of him. He could strangle her without a thought.

Colin arrived with her tea.

"Oh thank you, darling," she said, her hummingbird hand reaching out and caressing his cheek as he set the drink down.

"Is everything all right?" he asked.

"Of course, dear," she said. "You worry too much."

"I'll be down the hall if you need me," he said, leaving them with a small backward glance. He left the door open.

"How was your relationship with the kids?" he asked, measuring every word.

"It was great," she said, her thin lips smiling, missing teeth revealed again. "They were so appreciative of what we did for them. They became a part of our family."

"Hold her down," she said, her voice cold. "Face down on the bed."

The two kids did as she said, holding the smaller girl down. She was naked from the waist down.

"Don't let go, or you'll be next," she said. She held a thin metal rod, and as she moved, it flexed in her hand. The smaller girl struggled, but the older boy and girl were too strong for her.

She stood next to her, and brought the rod down on the back of her thighs, a small whistling noise filling the air before a sickening THACK rang out as the metal struck her flesh. The child screamed.

"We own you," she said. She beat her again, and again, and again. THACK THACK THACK. She was screaming, no words, just sobs and pain and terror.

"We'll send you back, and you'll live in a hole in the ground," she said. THACK THACK THACK.

"Never any problems with them?" he asked.

"What do you mean?" she asked, looking at him, taking a sip of tea, the cup trembling in her hand.

"With behavior or discipline," he said. *THACK THACK THACK.*

"Almost never," she said. "They came from so little. They always wanted to please us."

Truth screamed inside of him, and he stopped to breathe. He would do it, he would kill this woman and this would be the end. No one would know, no one would know the truth, he needed to breathe, breathe—

"I remember you," she said. "You were a reporter."

"Yes," he said. "I visited your home a few times."

"Your wife," she said. "She was lovely. How is she?"

"She's great," he said, trying to plaster the genuine smile back on his face, but failing.

"Oh, that's good to hear," she said. "Healthy marriages are hard to come by. It is what many people don't understand about me and Charlie. It is more than a marriage. It's a partnership. We work together on everything."

Leo looked into her eyes again. *Is* a partnership?

"Have you talked to Charlie yet?" she asked, smiling again. "He would love to hear about the book."

"No," said Leo. "Not yet. You think he's free?"

"He might be," she said. "You should check his study. He spends most of his time there."

His heart was racing, and Truth backed off, away.

"Could I go there now?" he asked.

"Shouldn't be a problem," she said, setting down her tea-cup. "Colin," she said, her voice the same low rasp, but he was there, in a moment.

"Could you show Mr. Price to Charlie's study?" she asked, looking up at him.

"Are you sure?" he asked.

"Of course I am, darling," she said. "Show him the way. And then come back here. I'll need some help shortly."

Leo grabbed his notebook and recorder, and followed Colin, leaving Barbara behind, crooked and bent.

The study was on the third floor, and up another flight of stairs. Colin led him to one of many doors and opened it for him, revealing a room filled with shelves, a massive desk on one side, covered in stacks of books and papers. It was a time capsule. Leo allowed himself a small smile.

"Has no one been in here since his death?" asked Leo.

"Not to my knowledge," he said. "Barbara refused anyone access, up until now. I've got to take care of her. I'll leave you to it." And Colin was gone, and Leo was alone, exactly where he needed to be.

Still, best to move fast. Find what was vital, and get out, before Barbara remembers that Charlie has been dead for over a decade.

There was so much. It looked like they had taken all of his papers and books that were left in the house and confined them to this room. The shelves overflowed, with stacks on the floor. The books he could discount, but the papers wouldn't be so easy. There could be evidence on them, and perhaps something valuable or useful to him.

The camera was the holy grail. Leo needed that more than anything. The camera first.

Where could it be? He looked over the shelves that bordered every wall of the room. There were miscellaneous things scattered everywhere. Folders, notebooks, old everything. He systematically went from shelf to shelf, leaving nothing unturned. Anywhere it could be hiding.

He could hear Colin's voice filter up from below in the house, as he took care of Barbara. Leo assumed Barbara was speaking back. Her low rasp wouldn't make its way up to him.

Nothing in the shelves. Doubt was rising in his mind. Maybe it wasn't here, perhaps it was destroyed or thrown away. It could be buried under tons of garbage in a landfill.

The desk, Leo.

Truth calmed him, her anger and rage pushed aside. She saw the end and forgot the immediate need for justice.

He rummaged through the many drawers of the desk. It was massive and heavy, beautiful and expensive. He emptied the drawers. One by one, he dumped the contents onto the floor.

Nothing but supplies, envelopes, print outs of old emails, garbage.

One drawer left. It was locked.

It must be inside. The key could be anywhere. He pulled on it, the lock holding strong. He yanked hard on it. The desk rattled loudly. Would they hear? Didn't matter, he needed in. He would knock down this damn house with his bare hands if that's what it took.

His shoulder burned as he pulled back and forth on it with all his might, the heavy wood shaking. He tugged and pulled. The handle came off in his fist with one final yank.

Fuck this. He stood up, raising his foot in the air, and kicked at the corner of the wood, hitting it with the heel of his boot as hard as he could, over and over. The wood splintered, and then the corner of the drawer broke. He shoved a hand inside and wrenched the door off. The contents spilled onto the floor.

Where was it where was it

Nothing but more papers, more garbage. On his hands and knees, he threw everything aside, hoping it was there, it *must* be there. Colin's voice echoed up from the floor below. His words were unintelligible. Panic rose in Leo. He would go room to room until he found the damn thing. He'd knock Colin unconscious, rip through the whole house, do whatever was necessary.

And then it was there, in his hands. It was massive, a reminder of how far they came in the intervening two decades with digital photography. His fingers searched every crevice of the device, looking for where the memory card was stored. Was it still there? Did it still have the evidence he needed?

The doorbell was ringing, but Leo ignored it as he found the memory card. He popped it out and pulled out his laptop, sliding it into the right adapter. He had bought out the electronics store the day before.

It auto opened, and the card was full, with dozens of images. They were loading. Loading. Colin answered the door below, the sounds echoing throughout the house. Someone was there.

The pictures loaded, finally. They were proof of everything.

He moused through them. Some showed nothing but shadow, some were only men grouped together, but more showing Barbara and Fred again. Charlie had taken photos from different angles, showing penetration and obscene close-ups. And then there were more, with the men from the room gone.

Wrong. Not all of them. A handful remained, and they were with one of the girls. It wasn't Ami, but another girl that Leo couldn't recognize, and then he closed the window. He couldn't see it because if he did he would rush down the stairs and beat elderly fragile Barbara to death with his bare hands and the truth would never come out.

He dumped them onto the laptop and small thumb drive he kept with him.

With the pictures found, he was there again. Leo could think. He was suddenly aware of his surroundings and he heard another conversation floating up from below. Colin was speaking to someone else, louder now. It wasn't Barbara, but a male voice. He stopped, walking to the door, sticking his head out to hear.

He's here, Leo.

Truth spoke to him, but he didn't need her, not this time. He could recognize the tone, as he had heard it twice before.

The cleaner was here. The man who ransacked his house, who threatened him, who strangled Trevor and god knows who else out in the swamp.

The killer was here for *him*.

20

Leo froze, panic hitting him hard. His feeling of invincibility had vanished. He moved.

Only the pictures mattered. He got his laptop. Upload them to the cloud, and then get out of here.

There was no internet here. *The old lady didn't need wi-fi, Leo.* He could tether it to his damn phone. Where the hell was it in the menu again? He scrolled through his settings, as the voices echoed up to him. They stayed below, for now. He couldn't hear what they said. What was the cleaner's play? He had followed him here. Or he had staked him out. The killer wanted the pictures, and Leo.

Goddamnit, why wasn't this working? The phone's network didn't show up on his laptop, fucking goddamn bastard thing. He didn't have time for this. The cleaner was coming for him. He needed to get out with the evidence.

But if the cleaner grabbed him, they'd be gone. The cleaner would destroy everything. That wasn't acceptable. Leo unplugged the thumb drive and capped it. He hoped it would protect it. It was small enough. He opened his jaw wide.

Down the hatch. He slipped it into his mouth and coated it with saliva. Before he could overthink it, Leo swallowed. It stuck for a moment in his gullet, sufficient time for Leo to picture them finding his body here, choked to death on a memory stick. But then it slid down his throat. A tight fit, but it made it. It was safe for now.

He packed his laptop away in his small bag, and left the room, peeking out, looking up and down the hall. No sign of the cleaner, but the voices from below were quiet. Was he sweeping through the house, searching for him? He wouldn't shoot him here. It'd be too much of a mess.

Leo couldn't jump from the third floor. He would break his legs, and then he'd be up shit creek. Still, he checked every door as he walked down the corridor, back toward the stairs. All of them were locked and all were heavy wooden doors. He would scurry out onto the roof if he could, but there wasn't a single window on this story, not from the hallway at least.

He got to the stairway, and crept halfway down, listening, watching, waiting. Leo heard no noise and saw no one in the hall. Wait, something on the second floor. Barbara doddered in her sitting room. Probably still sipping on her tea, wondering how Leo's conversation with Charlie was going. He had what he needed from her.

No windows on the middle floor either. All in the outside rooms, all the doors locked. Colin kept the place tidy. That's why the cleaner wasn't upstairs already. There was no way out. Leo needed to go through him to get out of there, and the cleaner knew it. He'd stay downstairs, could wait until the cows came home. Leo had to go down.

Maybe Barbara still had a use after all.

He walked back to the sitting room, where she softly hummed to herself. She sipped her tea, her mind off in another place.

"Ms. Collins," he said, quietly, walking up behind her.

She jumped. "You startled me," she said.

"It can't be helped," he said.

"Did you find Charlie?" she asked.

"Yes, I found him," said Leo. "I got exactly what I needed."

"Oh, perfect," she said.

"We need to go," he said.

"W—why?" she asked. "Colin should be right back."

"He's had an accident," he said. "It's an emergency. They want you downstairs, immediately."

"An accident?" she asked. "I—I can't walk the stairs anymore." She started to get up, her old body struggling. He helped her up, her arm trembling as it grabbed him.

"I'll carry you," he said. She was his ticket out of here. The cleaner wouldn't dare hurt her. He couldn't afford to.

Leo didn't know if she remembered her sins. Barbara spent years of her life putting up a facade. She wore masks as a lifestyle. As a hostess, as a politician's wife, and again as a serial rapist and abuser. She was practiced at hiding. She'd done it her whole existence. But when he looked into her foggy eyes, he couldn't tell what was real to her and what wasn't.

Did she remember the atrocities *she* committed? The ones she helped Charlie commit?

He didn't know.

But he didn't care. If she was hurt, if she died. He didn't care. The terror she could feel at being punished for a crime she didn't recall was small, incomparable to what she did to those children, over decades. She was disposable.

They needed to move before the cleaner sniffed out his plan. Barbara was up, on her feet, and he scooped her up into his arms, his pack slung around his back. She weighed nothing. He carried a bag of bones.

"Please be careful, darling," she said. "My constitution is not what it once was."

He said nothing in return. He wanted to dump her over the railing, and he could feel Truth's influence, as his grip tightened on her skin. She would have bruises.

She complained, but he didn't listen, as he began his way down the stairs to the first floor. He turned away from the large room for entertaining. He retraced his steps through a maze of hallways to the path out. The cleaner was waiting for him at the front door.

Leo put her down, sliding his forearm around her neck, pulling her close to him. He used her meager body as much of a shield as he could. He had no weapon, but he was as dangerous as a knife to Barbara.

"Oh Leo," said the cleaner. "Using an old lady as a hostage. Has it really come to this?"

He saw the cleaner, in the flesh, for the first time. He was big, six foot one and thick. Overweight, but Leo knew there was muscle behind that fat. His face was gentle with a cop's mustache. His eyes were easy, and his black hair was thinning and wispy. He wore khakis and a plain black polo. He had a pistol holstered on his side.

Leo had seen him before, as he tortured Trevor. The memory had faded away, but there was no doubt this was the same man.

"What is happening?" asked Barbara, weakly struggling against Leo.

"Don't worry, ma'am," said the cleaner. "This guy is a wanted criminal. I'm going to take him into custody, and everything will be a-okay."

"Is that how you got in here?" asked Leo. "Feeding people a bunch of bullshit."

"That hurts, Leo," he said. "And it's not bullshit. I do believe you're trespassing right now. Assault and battery on an elderly woman. Theft."

"Fuck you, killer," said Leo, over Barbara's shoulder. The cleaner's face remained calm, and his pistol stayed in his holster. He blocked the door.

"I don't know what you're talking about," he said.

"Get out of the way or I snap her neck," said Leo.

"Can't do that, Leo," he said. "You realize that."

"You will," he said, walking closer to him, holding Barbara's throat tight.

Break it show him

The cleaner reached to his pistol and thumbed off the catch.

"No one listens," he said, wrapping his fingers around the grip. "I tell people, over and over again. Simple, simple rules. Don't do this, don't do that, and everything will work out. And they just don't listen. It's frustrating, Leo."

"Don't," he said, pushing closer.

The cleaner pulled his pistol, hanging loose in his hand. "I told you. I said to drop it, and you'd have your life, have it all. And now we're here. You did this, not me. You made the choice to come here after I told you not to."

"You point that gun at me and she dies," said Leo. Barbara murmured something and started crying.

"Look at what you're doing," he said.

"She deserves far worse," said Leo.

"You're not gonna kill her, Leo," he said. "You don't have it in you. I can tell."

"You don't know what's inside me," said Leo. He couldn't get any closer. They were at an impasse.

The cleaner raised his pistol, pointed it at Leo, at Barbara.

"You can't risk hitting her," said Leo. "That's a mess even you can't clean up."

"I could find a way," said the cleaner. "I've had worse."

"I'm going to say it one last time," said Leo. "Move." He grabbed Barbara's throat even tighter. He could feel the give in it, feel how easy it would be to kill her now, end this now *do it*

Something in the cleaner's face changed, a tightness releasing.

"Okay, Leo," he said, lowering his pistol and sliding it into its holster. "I'm moving out of the way. Please don't hurt her. She doesn't deserve any of this. She's just an old lady." He put his hands up, and started sidestepping away from the door, and then his eyes looked off of Leo, behind him, and there was a sharp crack of pain in the back of Leo's head, and then darkness.

Flashes of light. Leo was on the ground, in the foyer, foggy. What happened? His arms pulled behind him and he struggled, handcuffs around his wrists.

Colin was there. He was talking to the cleaner, shaking his hand.

"You did a good job kid," said the cleaner. "He is a threat, as long as he's out in the public. Imagine using an old lady as a human shield."

"He seemed so honest," he said. "It was my fault, letting him in here in the first place."

"That's what he did for a living," said the cleaner. "Putting on a trustworthy face while he lies through his teeth. You did the right thing, in clocking him like that."

"Wish I could have done more," said the kid. "Poor Ms. Collins."

"Don't you worry," he said. "He won't be hurting anyone anymore."

His vision collapsed into darkness.

Another flash of light. He was lying in the back of a police car.

No, not police. The cleaner's. Leo sat up, his head aching. He had a concussion for sure. Leo squinted to keep out the glare. He could feel matted blood on the back of his head. The cleaner was driving down a highway Leo didn't recognize by sight. Metal grating separated the two.

"Back to the land of the living, I see," said the cleaner.

Leo said nothing. He launched a spray of saliva, some hitting the metal screen and some the cleaner. The cleaner grimaced, wiping his face off with a sleeve.

"Do not do that," he said. "The rest of your life will be very painful if you do that again."

"Fuck you," said Leo.

"This isn't my fault," he said. "I don't know why you're so angry at me. You only have yourself to blame. If you stayed in your own lane, none of this would have happened. You would be getting home from work right now, probably having your fourth drink of the night, watching your show. But instead, you are here."

Leo glared at the rearview mirror, into the cleaner's eyes as he stared back at him.

"This is the end, Leo," he said. "How in the hell did you think it would go any other way?"

21

The cleaner was taking Leo to the swamp, where he would kill him.

He drove, glancing back at Leo from time to time. His hands held the steering wheel loosely. Classic rock hummed on low volume from the radio. The car was old, a formless sedan from the nineties.

Leo's head ached from where Colin hit him. He had been threatening his ward, and so the kid clocked him. Leo had been stupid. He should have looked for him.

And now he was here, on his way to die. The cleaner's route was circuitous, full of twists and turns, down local roads that Leo didn't know. He didn't care if Leo saw the road to his shack. Leo would never come back out.

"Tired of feeding the masses that shit, huh?" he asked,

out of the blue.

Leo said nothing. He reached out for Truth, but she was gone. A void inside of him. There was no aura, no fear, only absence. He didn't understand. He had done what she said, followed her every whim. A hollow opened up inside of him. She had abandoned him. A desperate coldness was filling the space where she once dwelled.

"Your show was good for a laugh," he said, continuing the conversation, without Leo participating. "But holy shit, the fact that so many took it seriously. Kinda scary."

Right when he needed her most. She was gone. She had given up on him. Onto somebody else, someone who wouldn't fail her. Someone who would succeed.

"For a working gig, though, seemed like a good one," he said. "Be on TV, be famous, get paid a lot. Can't believe you gave it up."

"She convinced me," said Leo, finally, quietly.

"Speak up, Leo," he said.

"She convinced me," he said, looking up now, at the cleaner. "She assured me. She proved to me the error of my ways. She showed the poison I was unleashing upon the world. She cleansed me of those toxins, and I only wanted to repay her in kind."

"Who is this?" he asked. "Your ex-wife?"

"No," he said, on the verge of tears. "Truth."

"Ooookay," he said. "I thought it was a typical crisis of conscience kind of thing, but this is a whole 'nother level."

"You wouldn't understand," he said. "You haven't felt her. Haven't been touched by her, both good and bad. I let her in. Allowed her to affect change in me.

"You probably should have just seen a doctor," he said.

"Gotten you some meds, made everything right as rain. That's what they did with my ma, back when she was having trouble with my dad. Got her some pills, and she was her old self again."

"I'm not crazy," he said.

"Of course not," said the cleaner. "But you say that Truth showed you the way. Where is she now? Where has she been all this time? Those pictures are ancient, Leo. Charlie Collins has been dead for twelve years! Who are you going to punish? That old lady? Life punished her. She doesn't even know what day it is at this point, and can't piss without that kid helping her."

"The others," said Leo. "They all knew, and they did nothing. They let it all happen."

"And they deserve their lives ruined because of it?" he asked. "Because they didn't jump in and say something, about these powerful people that might have hurt them with that power. They were afraid, Leo. Doesn't seem fair to me."

"The Truth is intrinsic," he said.

"What are you even saying?" asked the cleaner. He turned off a highway, onto a two-lane road. The light was fading, and the center line faded in and out, decades-old paint wearing away. "You some philosopher or something? Everybody lies, all the time. My old man hit my mom, but I don't go broadcasting that on Facebook. Isn't my place."

"Everyone should know," said Leo, assured. They should all see. Truth deserved it. Those kids deserved it. Even if she was gone. Doesn't change anything.

"No one's gonna know, buddy," he said. "There's no coming back from where I'm taking you."

Leo's heart was bursting. "How can you do the things you do? These poor people. They just wanted to be heard."

"It's business, Leo," he said. "Like your show. In my experience, whoever I visit, they usually deserve my attention. They poked their nose where it didn't belong. They stole something. They want to hurt somebody. Your friend Trevor. He took something, something he was *expressly* forbidden to. He did it anyway, and then he gave it to you."

"Monster," said Leo, tears running down his face. "You kill for money."

"I correct mistakes," he said. "There are no innocents. Have you stopped and thought about how many people have died because of your show, Leo? Those reports you run, blaming this person and that. Stoking people's anger like you do. Or did. You don't anymore." He laughed. "That hatred has to be let out somewhere. How many wives were beaten because of angry husbands? Or kids? How many arguments flared up into fights, and even deaths, because of you? How many millions watched The Truth, over the years?"

Leo sat in silence.

"I've killed a few handfuls of people. I'd bet less than you, easy." He looked back in the rear view mirror, at Leo. "So who deserves what?"

He turned off the two-lane street, dusk settling in. The tires splashed through mud as they weaved their way down a narrow dirt road, trees encroaching on both sides. The headlights cut through the dark. They drove for miles down the muddy road and then the cleaner stopped, nothing but darkness ahead of them.

"Pencils down," he said, killing the engine. "No more

discussion."

He got out of the car, walking around to the other passenger door with his gun drawn. He opened Leo's door and Leo turned, and kicked it as hard as he could, with both feet. It hit the cleaner. He fell backward, stunned.

Leo was ready, contorting his arms, and brought them back underneath his legs. His knees and shoulders screamed in pain, but he ignored it. He'd need his arms free to have a chance. The cleaner tried to close the door, and Leo kicked it again. It struck the cleaner and he dropped to a knee one more time. Leo slid out of the car. He had to get the pistol.

The cleaner was on his butt. Leo dove for his gun. This fucker would pay. His hands were on it, wrenching it away from him, and then his head was rocked, as the cleaner drove his knee into Leo's temple, once, twice, three times. Leo was down. His head was ringing, screaming in pain.

The cleaner got up, and then there was a rope around Leo's neck. A noose, just like Trevor. It tightened. Leo coughed. He tried to get a finger in between it and his throat, but he failed.

"Did you think that would work?" asked the killer. "Did you really think that would work on me? I've seen everything, every trick in the book. I wanted to make it easy, but you're trying my patience."

He pulled Leo up and marched him along. Leo grabbed the rope with two hands, hoping to steal a few extra breaths as he was dragged. He was going to die like this, just like Trevor. Trees and swamp passed by his peripheral vision. Water seeped up into his shoes, his socks wet, splorching with every step.

He tried to beg for help, but all of his sound was cut off

by a tug of the noose.

"It's a shame," he said. "It didn't have to come to this."

So familiar. He had heard this before.

They marched for another minute and stopped at the edge of the water, stagnant, dark muck that buzzed with mosquitoes. Truth had shown him this. He had thought it was Trevor but it wasn't, it was him, she had tried to warn him, he hadn't seen it—

"Sorry, buddy," he said. "Time to die."

The cleaner began to tighten the noose, and Leo couldn't breathe. He tried to pull, struggled, but there was no fight in him. His brain was dying, his heart failing. The rope tightened. This was it. He pulled away with what little strength he had left.

"Stop your struggling," said the killer, straining, his chest heaving. "I've done this enough times. There's no way out. This is the end."

And then the killer fell over him, tumbling over Leo's kneeled body, the rope flying out of his hands. The tension on the noose eased and Leo caught a giant gasping breath. He yanked it away from the cleaner. The cleaner was face first in the mud. Leo loosened the noose enough to breathe, and then jumped on the back of the cleaner. Leo's two hundred plus pounds hit him hard, driving the air out of him. Leo wrapped the chain of the handcuffs around his neck and pulled, wrenching the cleaner's head back, choking him, screaming in rage.

"Stop your struggling," said Leo. "There's no way out. This is the end."

He plunged the killer's head forward, into the muck. Leo forced his face into the wet mud. Leo put his weight into it, the cleaner floundering, but unable to get Leo off of him.

"No one will know you died," he said. "No one will find your body. You'll rot out here in the swamp, alone."

The cleaner struggled, making muffled grunts into the sludge, and then he stopped moving, dead. Leo held him there for another thirty seconds for good measure, and then let go. He rolled off of him, covered in muck and sweat. He ran through the cleaner's pockets and found the handcuff keys. He undid the cuffs and threw them aside.

He wiped his hands as much as he could and then jammed two fingers down his throat, hitting his gag reflex. He pushed further and he vomited bile and acid.

He did it again, and he puked again, stomach acid coming up through his nose and mouth. He spat it out and tried one more time. He dry heaved once, but then it came, the memory card. He wiped off the bile and pocketed it.

And then Truth was there again. He could feel her, her golden aura, warming him from the cold swamp water.

"It was you," he said. "You helped me. You threw him."

She didn't speak, but he felt her assent. He felt the warmth fill him. Leo had suffered for her, and she had repaid in kind. She embraced him and the aching pain in his head, throat, and wrists was gone. She soothed all his ills.

He looked over at the cleaner, lying dead in the muck. Leo looted the corpse, pocketing the cash and keys. He grabbed his cell phone and threw everything else into the swamp, as far as he could, leaving the body.

Leo went back to the car and sat behind the wheel. He breathed. He was covered in mud, bruises raising around his throat and wrists. Truth retreated into him and the pain swelled like a symphony. He had gotten the pictures, and he had eliminated a threat. He had demonstrated his faith in Truth.

He opened up the phone and scrolled through the contacts. Thousands of them. Still, Leo found the one he was looking for. He dialed.

It rang, seven or eight times, but someone picked up, right before voicemail.

"I told you not to call me at this number," said Adam Simonson. "I'm in the fucking middle of dinner with my family.

Leo paused, letting the silence sit.

"Smith? Hello? Was there a problem?" he asked, a stage whisper.

Leo spoke, finally.

"Truth is coming for you."

22

"Price?" asked Simonson. "Where's Smith?"

"Don't know that name," said Leo. "But there's a dead man out here in the swamp that might have answered to it. He never gave me yours, though. I knew it was you. You have the most to lose."

"You stupid son of a bitch," said Simonson, bitterness pouring out of the phone. "Do you think this is the end of it?"

"No, it'll end with you resigning," said Leo. "You'll probably avoid jail time, and maybe any civil suits that spring up, but there's no way you'll keep your job. And you can kiss the presidency goodbye. Attending gang rapes of underage African kids? I don't think even *your* constituency will abide that."

Simonson sputtered and then found his voice. "One old picture doesn't prove a thing, and you know it. Release that photo, and the media will tear it apart. You stupid bastard. You've thrown your whole life away over a single printout."

Charlie Collins sat across the desk from him. It was big, heavy, solid wood. It was the desk of a senator. Simonson was anxious, but he projected confidence, even at his young age. Charlie leaned back in his chair, sizing up the kid. Charlie was younger then, with a streak of black in his gray hair.

"You've done a lot in a short amount of time," said Charlie.

"I don't believe in wasting it," said Simonson.

"I've noticed," said Charlie. "What do you want, Adam?"

"What do you mean?" he asked.

"What's your ambition? Your goals?" asked Charlie. "Do you want to be a Senator? Secretary of State? President?"

"I want to lead the country," he said. He smiled. He thought he knew what that meant at the time.

Leo didn't flinch, not anymore, when Truth showed him things. He was her conduit, her vessel. Whatever she gave him, he took.

"What about hundreds of pictures?" asked Leo. "There's one in particular that features a nice close-up of you. Hard to argue it's anyone else, especially considering your relationship with Charlie Collins. He was a mentor of sorts for you, wasn't he? I remember you following him around like a lost puppy dog in Washington, ready to lap up any treat that dropped off the grown-up's table."

"You bastard," he said. "You're lying."

"Nope," said Leo, unable to stop himself from smiling. He hoped Simonson could hear the smile, talking on his phone, in a back room of his house, while his kids and wife ate a nice dinner, his growing cold on the plate. "Charlie Collins never erased those pictures off of that dinosaur of a digital camera. He was old, and he got away with it under so many noses for so many years. And now I have all of them. Pretty vile stuff."

"You motherfucker," said Simonson. "I'll—"

"Send another killer after me?" asked Leo. "This one failed. Not becoming of a future president, I would say."

Simonson sputtered again. "N—now Price," he said. "It doesn't have to be this way. We don't have to be enemies."

"We don't?" asked Leo. "I've lost my job. Damn near killed. Because of you."

"It's easy," said Simonson. "Smith? Who cares? He lived on the fringe. Forgotten already. No one will miss him. Your job? Could be yours again, with a single phone call. After we hang up, you're the lead of The Truth again. Stahlbock? Back on a bus to Omaha or wherever the fuck he's from. You have your life again, good as new. Better than new."

"Did you like the party?" asked Charlie. It was the Monday after.

"Your wife is an excellent host," he said. "I know it must be hard to orchestrate those things, but it felt seamless."

"She's very talented," said Charlie, smiling.

"About your party," said Simonson.

"Yes?" asked Charlie, raising an eyebrow.

"A little birdie told me that there's an invite-only after party," he said.

"And you want in?" asked Charlie.

"So you're not denying it?"

Charlie's smile dimmed. He stared hard at Simonson, studying him. "I don't think you're ready."

"I'm ready," he said. "What would I not be prepared for?"

"It's—it's sensitive," said Charlie. "And not everyone can deal with it. It's led to some—ugliness—in the past. I'd hate for that to happen to you."

"Don't worry about me," said Simonson. "I can handle it. I want to move up."

Charlie looked at him a second longer and then nodded. "Alright. You're in."

"I don't want my job back," said Leo. "I don't want my life. It was poison."

"I'm just spitballing, Price," said Simonson. "You can have anything. You can retire as a 'political consultant' for the rest of your days. Go live on the beach and fuck twenty-year-olds until you die."

"Whatever I want?" said Leo.

"Whatever you want," said Simonson. "Make those pictures disappear, and I can get you anything. Money, fame, power. I *will* be president. No doubt about it. And after that, all bets are off. You want a position in my cabinet, you've got it. You can do what you want, and no one can stop you. Travel the world on the government's dime."

Simonson leaned against the wall, looking as the African kid thrust into Barbara. The first few of these "secret events" he attended he felt weird and awkward, but now it just business as usual. Watching a black kid fuck Charlie Collins' wife did nothing for him, certainly not like it did for Charlie. But to be here was to be important, was to be elite. And if this was the cost? So be it.

"What if what I want is to reveal the truth and punish everyone who stayed silent while children were raped?"

"You want your story?" Simonson asked. "Fine. Publish it. Keep me out of it. I've worked too hard and too long to get where I'm at. I will be the President, mark my words, and I won't let Charlie Collins dumb dead ass ruin it for me. You want to reveal the truth? Fine. You want to punish everyone there? I'll give you the names, Leo. I will make sure every single one of them is dragged through the wringer, lose everything they had. Just leave me out of it."

Simonson followed Charlie down a corridor.

His guts were tight. Was it anxiety? Or was it excitement?

"I'm glad you've made it this far, Adam," said Charlie. They walked down the hallway.

His palms were sweaty. He wiped them off on his slacks. They approached a door, much like all the other doors. Charlie grabbed the knob, held it in his hand, paused a moment.

"She's waiting for you," he said. "Have fun."

Charlie opened the door, and she was there, sitting on the edge of the bed, staring at the floor. She wore a simple dress, white and clean. She turned and glanced at him, her face empty, eyes resigned.

Simonson looked at her and walked inside.

"That sounds great," said Leo. "Except the truth doesn't make exceptions. Black and white. Wrong and right. Nothing in between. And you'll be counted, just like the rest."

"Please, Leo," said Simonson, his voice a harsh whisper. "I am begging you. This will ruin me. It will destroy my entire life."

"I wonder if those children begged. I'm sure they did. I doubt it earned them any mercy," said Leo.

"You can't—"

"I can, and I will," said Leo. "If it's the last thing I do."

"You fucking idiot," said Simonson, launching invectives. "You think Smith is all I can do? They'll find you, and they will bury you so deep the whole world'll forget you existed. I will be President, Price, I will, and you and those goddamn pictures won't stop me, I'm going to ki—"

Leo hung up. He turned off the phone, got out of the car, and tossed it into the bog. It splashed in the distance, somewhere out in the dark water.

He found the shack. Truth knew where it was, and she guided him to it. It was almost empty, a chair and a light bulb all that remained inside.

Leo thought to find Trevor, but the swamp was endless. His body could be anywhere. He grabbed the ankles of the cleaner and dragged him into the shed. Leo was already covered in mud. A little more wouldn't hurt him.

A small can of gasoline was in the trunk. He emptied it, pouring it over the remains of the cleaner, upending it. He choked on the fumes, but he dumped out the whole thing. The cheap wooden floor soaked through.

He lit a match and threw it in. The building ignited, thick black smoke rising into the air.

Leo watched it burn, sitting on the hood of the car. Truth observed the blaze with him. He could feel how much it pleased her. She was hungry.

The thin walls collapsed. The fire eventually burned itself out.

He left, the body and the shack still smoldering behind him.

23

Leo left the swamp, driving the cleaner's car out. He needed space, and time, if he wanted to break the story right. Simonson wouldn't give him either. Despite what he had said on the phone, Leo knew he would not rest on his laurels. There'd be more men after him.

Leo went to a full-service truck stop first. He bought a change of clothes, and then showered, throwing his old clothes away.

He drove the cleaner's car to the airport, parking in the longterm lot, in the middle. It was another car of thousands. Maybe they'd find it, but nobody would report the cleaner missing. No one wanted him found. He left it and walked to the rental area. Got a nondescript sedan, and paid for it in cash.

The rental would do for now. There was a strip of hotels, an exit down from the airport. Leo chose the one tucked furthest back from the road. The chain motel did its best to appear clean. He paid for a room along the backside and reversed the car so the license plate wasn't visible.

It was late. The last vestiges of the adrenaline wore off, ebbing out of Leo's body. He laid down in the cold, hard bed. Truth softened and warmed it. He slept like the dead. Leo woke up after noon.

And then he worked.

Leo ventured out and got breakfast. He bought himself *another* new laptop, identical to the one laying at the bottom of a swamp somewhere.

He set up his impromptu office at the shitty desk in his room. The lighting was terrible, but it would do. He grabbed his previous notes from the cloud and started a new file, up-loading all the data from the memory card, still intact after its ride inside his guts.

He went through the pictures. They numbered in the hundreds. Leo organized them, trying to stay removed as the horror washed over him.

Shots of insertion, of body parts. They had no real value, other than demonstrating abuse. A folder for them. A siz-able amount.

Any photo with visible faces. Leo separated them into their own folder, dozens of them. He pulled up images of the children, opened every picture of Charlie Collins from the time, from his office, from newspapers covering his charity, Barbara's parties, all the associated hangers-on, and those in Charlie's inner circle.

Leo compared.

Every person was a mystery. Finding identities with the modern internet made it easier and faster, with heaps of data a few key presses away. The hours of the day passed behind him and Leo put names to faces.

With some, he found no name, no face to face comparison. Others, he was sure were bit players, obscure then and even more mysterious now. They still deserved punishment. He couldn't find them, couldn't reach them. Not yet.

Moreover, for others, he discovered their identities. Their faces printed in old newspapers, in publicity shots shaking Charlie Collins' hand, big smiles plastered onto them. But like Charlie, they already burned in hell for their crimes.

But more still, like Adam Simonson, were active in government, as consultants, as judges, as lawyers, as leaders of men. Not only were they active, continuing on from those complicit days, but thriving. Using Collins as a handhold, to climb higher. Utilizing the brotherhood of rape to move further in the world.

Leo worked. He built a spreadsheet, cross-referencing names, faces, demonstrating the direct evidence he had, and what they did.

Photo after photo in front of him, and the rage from Truth grew inside him, even as he tried to control it. She was a phoenix, full of fire and anger and death. He could feel it burning within him, wanting to break free. The wraith that once haunted him was straining underneath his skin. She stretched at the bounds of him.

But he didn't stop. The work was too important. He required every name and face. Leo needed them to confront the truth of what they did, even as the rage threatened to burn him up. The names accrued. Senators, judges, lawyers, consultants, and conglomerates, all represented. All older now, some like Simonson, entering the prime of their political careers. Others, aging out, facing retirement.

All would know shame.

The guilty weren't the only he identified. The children were there as well, not just Fred. He saw Ami and two other girls. He thought they were Dalia and Latrice. Their ages lined up, and they were the latter four kids, the last to age out and leave. They both lived out of state, Dalia in California, Latrice in France.

The fire burned hotter as Truth looked at the images. Even with the AC turned up high Leo sweat, the once cold wraith turned to flames. In minutes his shirt was soaked through, smoke rising in his lungs.

He would burn alive. Truth's rage would consume him.

He was almost done with today's work. He pored through them all, organized them, filed them away, the sorrow and abuse sorted and stacked. Leo saved them to his computer, to the cloud, to a third backup, another computer, another email address. There would never be enough copies.

Leo coughed, and he gulped down water, trying to forestall Truth's anger. He was almost done for the day. There was one last thing to do.

His encounter with the cleaner showed him he was not enough. If they took him, there was no backup. He copied all his data, all his notes, and wrote an email.

Diana,

They're after me. If something happens, here's my story. Do what you can.

- Leo

He coughed again, and he couldn't stop. The coughs racked his body. Smoke and rage filled him. He was stupid, thinking he could fill himself with all the horror those photos contained with no reaction from Truth. Leo thought he could soldier through it, pay the price of those images in his mind, and try and swallow them down, force them aside when he slept. That alone would be hard, but he hadn't come this far to back away from it.

Truth was a different story. She was burning him up, with no thoughts to his limits or his body. He gulped another long gulp of ice water, but it did nothing to chill the rage. He threw off his sweat soaked clothes, and turned on the shower, flipping the lever until cold water shot from the nozzle. He got underneath it, shocking him at first, but then feeling good, a relief from the heat. The coughing subsided, the icy water cooling him down. He could breathe again.

PUNISH

KILL

BURN

She raged inside him, even as the frigid water kept him alive.

"We will," he said, his voice echoing in the motel bathroom. "We will hurt them. I'll hold them accountable. They'll face justice. But you have to stay in control. I'll die, and the truth will die with me."

She didn't answer, but he could sense the heat inside him ebb.

"I won't forget," he said. "I have you now. And together, we will make them feel shame."

The fire dissipated, and the cold water chilled him. He turned the temperature up, degree by degree, and then got out, still breathing hard. Truth vanished within him some- where, into the spot where she retreated and rested. Her rage had exhausted her. And him. He was suddenly drained, the day's work of researching and enduring those photos taking everything out of him.

He threw on pajamas, looking through the curtains. Nothing. No men sitting in parked cars waiting for him. No headlights.

He laid down in bed and flipped on the television. Dreck and worthless garbage. Headlines flashed across the screen with every news station. The Truth would be on in a few minutes. A part of him was curious, wanting to know what the show was doing with John in the lead. Was it more "hu- man interest" stories? More lemonade stands and gentle reports of indoctrination? Would Warren work his magic on John, just like he did with Leo, and force him to see the light?

He turned off the TV. The show had been *him*, for so, so long, but now, he wanted nothing more than to forget it and make everyone forget his association with it.

Plans. He got out a notebook and laid out his ideas for building the story. He'd call the two other girls, tell them what he had found, and hope they would cooperate. Then the other kids.

He thought to interview some of those faces he identi- fied. Make them squirm, defend themselves. But the less who knew the better, until it came out, and their lives were gone, in a flash. It was the justice they deserved. No prepa- ration. No plan. Their identity as monsters revealed in an instant.

His burner phone buzzed on the nightstand next to him.

He didn't recognize the number. He answered.

"Hello?" he asked. Was it another cleaner, some hitman out to bury him in the swamp?

"Mr. Price?" asked the voice. It sounded familiar. Leo couldn't place it.

"Who is this?" he asked, not answering.

"It's Fred," said the voice. "I want to talk."

24

The anger and the outrage was all gone from Fred. In their place was a desperate sadness, one that poured out from him, gaining strength as Leo spent time with him.

They met in Leo's motel room, the day after Fred called him. Fred sat in the lone chair in the room, while Leo remained on the edge of the bed. Leo's phone recorded their conversation. He scribbled notes as fast as he could.

Fred was looking through the photos, with Leo's laptop on the table, clicking through each photo, his face a mask. He didn't reject them, like their initial encounter. He absorbed them, and the pain they caused. It was the first thing he requested when he got there. Was to look through the pictures.

Leo said nothing. He only watched Fred as he clicked

through every single image.

"What changed?" asked Leo. "Why talk to me now?"

"Ami called me," he said, not taking his gaze off the screen. "And told me you drove up there to meet her. And that it was time for the truth to come out. That nobody would blame me for what happened."

There was something in Fred's eyes, that Leo couldn't pick out before.

"Were you close to Ami?" asked Leo.

"Yes and no," said Frederick. "We were the two closest in age, and we got along well. But mother and father, I mean, Charlie, and Barbara—they pitted us against each other. They kept us separate from each other, made sure that we never had time to talk at length. They knew if any of us revealed the truth, it was over. So they punished us. Rewarded the loyal ones, any who watched the others."

"Rewarded how?" asked Leo.

"Money," he said. "Clothes. Anything we wanted. I got a brand new Corvette on my sixteenth birthday. It was fire engine red. A beautiful, beautiful car. The way the girls at school looked at me when I pulled up in that. When I was a child, I never once thought that I would have a car like that. Would *live* like that."

"They trapped you," said Leo.

"Yes," he said. "They made the alternative worse. They never stopped reminding us of where we came from, and where we were now. That nothing in life was free, and we were merely paying a price."

"And you felt guilty?" asked Leo. "Complicit?"

"Yes. I watched my brothers and sisters beaten. They suffered because of me. Because I was afraid of returning. And if the truth came out—that's where we would go. To the orphanage. Back to poverty."

"Start from the beginning," said Leo. "When did it begin?"

"My first night there," he said. "It was very scary. I had never flown on a plane before, and then I was flying over the Atlantic. A limousine picked me up from the airport. They were both there when I arrived at the mansion. That gigantic mansion."

"How old were you?"

"Eleven," he said. "I had just turned eleven. We didn't receive real presents, but they told me about the adoption as a birthday present. And they both introduced themselves and the other kids to me, and they showed me the house."

"How many others were there?"

"There were four," he said. "At the time. Semmi was about to leave for college. They all said hello, but were otherwise silent. I thought it was because I was new. It wasn't."

Fred continued. "Then they brought me to my room, which was gigantic. I never had my own space in the orphanage. No privacy. I had shared everything. And here, I had a king-size bed in a massive bedroom, filled with toys and books. Books! I had never owned a book up until that moment. I had my own bathroom."

He was silent.

"Fred?" asked Leo.

"I took a shower, my first night there. And—and I didn't hear her open the door—I didn't hear Barbara come in, behind me, into the bathroom. She was wearing a robe, but by the time I saw her, she was naked, in there with me, touching me. I didn't know what to do. The woman who adopted me was suddenly showering with me? Touching me? I was shocked. And I froze. I let her touch me. I was eleven. I only kind of knew how sex worked. And when—when I was done, she left. I finished showering. I didn't know what to do."

"You were a kid," said Leo.

"It was only the beginning," he said. "And it led to more and more, and eventually led to the parties."

"The parties," said Leo. "Were they usually like that picture?"

"What do you mean?" asked Fred.

"Were there always that many people present?" asked Leo. "And was it always Barbara?"

"Yes," he said. "She wouldn't share me. Charlie liked sharing the girls and watching Barbara, but she never shared. And sometimes there was less. They came and went. Some were constantly there. You could tell they were the ones who enjoyed it. There were plenty who made token appearances just to receive father's favor. If they wanted a bill passed, if someone needed in on a subcommittee—they would accept his invitation, stand there, and then on Monday morning they'd get what they want."

"Do you think it was known in Washington? What happened at those after parties?"

"I don't know," he said. "Father inspired loyalty. The men who were there knew. And the parties themselves weren't a mystery. But nobody stopped them. No one objected."

"For years," said Leo.

"For years."

They talked for hours, Frederick answering every question. He stopped to compose himself a few times, but now

Leo had two of the children, with long interviews, with damning evidence.

"Do you think it's worth it?" asked Fred.

"Worth it?" asked Leo. He could feel Truth within him. The memories of the past few weeks rising up inside. The wraith, the beach, losing his job. Killing the cleaner in the swamp. There was no question in his mind. Of course it was worth it.

"Father is dead. Mother has dementia, and will surely pass soon."

"But what about all those who said nothing? Who let it happen?" asked Leo. "Don't you want to see them punished?"

"I was one of those people, Mr. Price," he said. "I allowed it to continue."

"You were a kid," said Leo. "They trapped you in a situation you couldn't possibly control." Fred was struggling. He had something he wanted to say, but Leo couldn't pull it out of him. After hours of discussion, he was keeping something from Leo.

"But I am not a child anymore," he said. "I'm a grown man, and their name is still mine. Everything I've done in life is connected to their name. My firm has its name attached to it. And when their name means something else— what happens to me? Charlie Collins was respected. Adored, even. Everyone loved him, and they still love his name. But when you break your story—they won't anymore. They'll see him as a monster, and his name as a name for monsters. Those men will not be the only ones punished. I will be punished too."

Leo studied Fred. His hands trembled, a slight shudder,

and Fred stopped it, squeezing his fists tight, before wiping away the tears in his eyes. Leo saw the guilt he was carrying. There was nothing he could say.

"I don't want to share a name with monsters," he said. "I'm sorry. Mr. Price. I shouldn't have come here. This was a mistake."

"Fred," said Leo, but Fred was already out the door, pulling his jacket on, and he was gone. Leo was alone again, and he turned off his phone recording. Frederick had turned on a dime, being open and honest with Leo. As soon as they started talking about the repercussions, he balked. Leo hadn't looked too deeply into the personal lives of the kids, as grown adults, but he'd have to do some digging. It might help explain Fred's behavior.

Leo couldn't understand it. Of course there was a cost for all of this, for unearthing the truth. Fred couldn't feel Truth like he could. Fred hadn't faced her down as she descended upon him, elongated pale body with a storm cloud of black hair, and Fred hadn't felt her warmth and care after Leo embraced her. Truth had saved Leo's life, and he would do anything to repay her. The truth was worth everything.

Leo took the notes from his interview with Fred, and entered them into his laptop, saving everything again, transcribing their conversation, typing for hours. The whole time he felt filled with righteousness, with Truth. She never left him anymore, and she filled his heart. She led, and he followed.

.

Four men came that night. They kicked down Leo's door, grabbing him from his bed, tying him up, gagging him. Someone slipped a black bag over his head.

They were fast, professional, and they knew exactly where he was.

25

The men didn't talk. They only brutalized.

They were fast, and Leo was unprepared. He thought he was safe again, in his motel room, with his rental car. He wasn't. They found him, and they took him.

He woke up when they kicked the door in, on his feet, bleary eyes struggling to see in the dark. They wore all black. The men were big, all taller, younger, and stronger than him. He grabbed a chair, swinging it wildly in front of him, but it was yanked away, and a steel baton hit him in the back of the knee, and he was down. One more to his neck, and he couldn't move, pain paralyzing him. He reached out to Truth, but she couldn't stop this. Or wouldn't.

They jerked his arms behind him, with a zip tie pulled taut around his wrists. The men forced a gag into his mouth, and then a black bag slid over his head. They pulled him up, not to his feet, but in the air. The agony in his neck lessened enough for him to fight, but they held him tight. Their grips were iron. They cinched their fingers onto his bones.

They carried him through the dark and then a sliding van door opened, and they dropped him.

"Don't move, or it'll hurt," said a voice, loud and deep. He believed the voice, and he didn't struggle. He was no escape artist, and these men were not like the cleaner. They didn't talk. They did their job.

An engine started and they moved. The metal floor vibrated.

They had found him.

He had done everything right. Ditched anything traceable, used a burner phone, spent cash. Still, they tracked him. How?

As Leo floundered on the floor of the vehicle, in the dark, it clicked.

Fred.

Leo had seen the look in Fred's eyes, the presence of guilt and pain. It wasn't wrong to assume that's what that look had represented.

It *was* wrong to assume that it was the guilt of a victim, of a person who blamed themselves for being abused.

It wasn't. It was the guilt of a man who wanted to keep his name clean. Desperate enough to make a deal with Adam Simonson. Desperate enough to sell another man's life away.

The look of guilt on his face. The value of his name. It wasn't a philosophical question or one of conscience. It was practical.

Fred hadn't talked to Ami. He had known Leo wouldn't

check. Simonson had gotten to him, influenced him, got in his ear. The trauma was buried, buried deep, and Fred didn't want to dig it up. And he'd kill any man who tried.

The van took a hard turn and he slid along the floor, into someone's leg. A short kick pushed him away, a stab of pain.

Truth was there. He could feel her there, holding, waiting. She hadn't warned him, not this time. Only her steady presence guiding him, but no visions and no ominous hallucinations. Which meant this is where Truth wanted him to be. Black bagged, bound, on the floor of a vehicle. Right where he was supposed to be.

So he didn't struggle, and he took the kick in the stride, confident knowing that Truth was leading him on the correct path. He knew her, and her guiding hand would take him to the right place.

It felt like days, down on the cold metal floor, in the darkness. The four men didn't say a word the entire journey. Leo swam in the dark expanse of empty time, his mind drifting away from the bottom of the van to the warm embrace of Truth. She held him there, in that black wilderness, her glowing aura monopolizing his vision. He saw her now, in her natural form, a luminous angel. The pale wraith was a long forgotten memory. Her shadow only came out in an hour of need. She floated there, in the void. White flowing robes matched her porcelain skin. Her hair surrounded them. It protected them. Her eyes, once full of rage, wide saucers of pain, were soft, accepting, perfect. Her mouth was closed. She didn't require words. Her touch said all she needed. This was the truest version of Truth, the truest because the truth was not ugly. Anyone who claimed otherwise didn't understand.

He was changed, a different man. It was all through her. She held his hand as they floated there, and pulled him in close to her. She held him, mother to son, with complete control and protection. Her touch was ambrosia, and his body was far from that metal floor. He felt only her embrace. She had him.

And then they stopped, and he was ripped out of the void, away from her grasp, back into the arms of the men. They dragged him out of the van, a jolt of pain roaring through him as he hit the pavement. They grabbed him, lifting him again. He didn't struggle. He was where he was needed.

They carried him, and then sat him in a chair. His zip ties were replaced with handcuffs, and he was cuffed to the chair by wrists and ankles. It was cold, the metal seat sucking the heat out of him. Truth restored it with her warmth.

"Soften him up," said a voice.

Then he was hit, a punch in the face, white stars in his vision, underneath the hood. And again, and again. He couldn't see them coming, and his head rang, first his lip bleeding, and then CRACK, his nose breaking. He could feel the blood flowing from it now, over his mouth, down his chin. Truth's warmth tried to absorb the pain, but it couldn't take it all, and Leo grunted and groaned as they beat him. Over and over again, and doubt crept in, beneath his skin, that this wasn't the right place or where he was needed.

"Enough," said the voice.

They stopped. There was quiet, peace, for a moment, long enough for Leo to feel the blood pouring from his broken nose, split lip, and eyebrow.

Then the hood was ripped off. He winced. The bright

lights blinded him. His eyes adjusted, red dripping, drip drip drip, over his left, and he saw where he was, right where he needed to be. It was a warehouse filled with crumbling shelves and rotting boxes. The men stood around him, two in front of him, and he assumed two behind.

"This is your fault," said the same voice, from the shadows. He stepped out. Simonson. He gestured at one of the thugs. "The gag. I want to talk to him."

One of the brutes took it out of Leo's mouth. He stretched his jaw as the blood flowed out of his split lip.

Simonson stood in a black tracksuit and sunglasses, staring down at him and smiling. He looked picture perfect. Always ready for a photo op, even at a murder. His hair was slicked back and his fingers manicured. Leo could see the crows feet, the stress wrinkles in his forehead, though. No makeup tonight. Leo had always thought Simonson resembled a muppet, and the effect was worse up close.

"Why didn't you listen, Leo?" he asked. "All you had to do was listen. Now look at us. Look where we are."

Leo spit a wad of blood, landing at Simonson's feet.

"Just short, Leo," he said. "Story of your life, huh?"

"I'm exactly where I need to be," said Leo, his voice grinding out of him.

"Is that right?" asked Simonson. "Hard for me to argue with that. It was close. You almost got away from me. After all that boy went through, he still took a deal. Sometimes a lie is more valuable than the truth."

"It's ugly," said Leo. Tears rolled down his face. "It's all so ugly."

That struck Simonson, and he stared at Leo in shock.

"What happened to you, Price?" he asked. "You were a

company man. You did good work. Why turn now? It boggles the mind."

Leo breathed, forcing air through his broken nose and mouth. "You wouldn't understand."

"I wouldn't understand what?" asked Simonson. "A crisis of conscience? Do you think I'm a monster, Leo? If I peel back my skin, is there something alien underneath? I hate to disappoint you, but I'm just like you."

"The old me," said Leo.

"That's true," said Simonson. "The old you was smarter. Knew when to keep his head down."

"Not smarter," said Leo, haggard. "A snake. Spewing venom."

"Ha," said Simonson. "You're not too wrong about that one, but nobody made you do the show, and sell all that stupid bullshit."

Leo looked down, his head too heavy. His ears were still ringing from the punches.

"I wanted to pay down my ledger," said Leo, struggling to speak.

"What was that?" asked Simonson, getting closer. "I can't hear you, Leo."

"I wanted to pay down my ledger," said Leo.

"Pay down your ledger?" asked Simonson. "What world are you living in? There's no such thing, Leo! Come on, man. No one is counting your sins. Everyone is dirty, Leo. Everything is sick."

"That's a lie," said Leo.

"Show it to me, then," said Simonson, shrugging. "Did those African kids upset you, Leo? It's nothing, a drop in the bucket. I know of worse, done by more important people than Charlie Collins. Our government is built on cover-ups, on hiding. And not just ours, all of them. And not just the government, everything. It is precarious secrets keeping this all glued together. And you'd pull it all apart."

"I want to show people the truth," said Leo. "They deserve it."

"If they saw the truth," said Simonson. "It would kill them. Their minds would shatter. They loved your bullshit, Leo, because it was a truth they could accept."

"No," said Leo, feeling Truth's warmth, rising in his chest. "Truth is intrinsic, inevitable. You, you can't fathom her, you never could. I was the same, but then she came into my heart and changed me. She *made* me recognize the difference, showed me her beauty. She will come for you, and make you understand. You'll see."

Simonson looked at him, long and hard, his eyes searching Leo's face. Leo stared back. Simonson sighed, finally.

"Sorry, Leo," he said. "Well, not too sorry." He nodded behind Leo, and there was a cord wrapped around his throat, and he couldn't breathe, and he struggled now, there was no way not to. His brain screamed, his lungs empty.

He was right where he needed to be, his vision starting to fade. Truth was here with him, he could feel her. She would help Leo, just like in the swamp. She would find him a path. He would still achieve her mission.

The cord tightened, and he could feel the blood from his wounds crawl down his face as he tried desperately to breathe, to pull the chair forward, to do something, but there was no escape.

He was right where he needed to be. Truth was there, her warmth filling him, padding his throat, the pain numbing, giving him all the air he needed. She would stop them. She would save him, save him again. It was what she did.

Leo's vision darkened further, and the cord pulled tighter. There was no air left.

Truth touched him in the darkness. She was a glowing angel and she brought him in tight, mother to son. He looked into her soft perfect eyes, and there was only approval, only love. She brought him even closer, embracing him with all she had. She comforted him. She warmed him. She held him as he died. Right where he needed to be.

Leo's body went slack.

Simonson watched. "I don't want him found. Ever. Bury him deep. And destroy all the evidence he had."

26

"Welcome once again, to The Truth. I'm John Stahlbock. Let's begin!"

John turned to the camera, his handsome face composed, assured. His brown eyes were comforting, welcoming, but then hardened, to first greet the viewer and then give them confidence in him. He had practiced the transition for hours in a mirror.

"We start tonight with bombshell news about the disappearance of our departed host, Leo Price. He disappeared nearly a month ago, after breaking into the house of former Senator Charlie Collins' widow, Barbara, and fleeing from the scene. This was after erratic behavior led to him being dismissed as anchor of this show."

John pivots, looking into the second camera.

"However, authorities have allegedly found his body, stuffed into a barrel, dredged up in an unrelated salvage mission in the Baltimore harbor. Police are investigating foul play. This comes on the heels of blockbuster accusations by Diana Walters, ex-wife of Price, reporting for the New York Times."

"Breaking last week, Walters report alleges a widespread conspiracy, starting with Charlie and Barbara Collins, involving dozens of other important figures in and around the Washington DC area. The story includes allegations of extensive sexual abuse toward Collins' adopted children, which were front and center for the Collins' charity work, spread over two decades. Adam Simonson, Speaker of the House, is the largest figure in the article, which states he was present for, and participated in, the sexual abuse."

The feed cuts to a shot of Simonson, visibly upset, talking to the camera. His voice is trembling, and a tear rolls down his cheek while he speaks.

"These allegations are hurtful, not only to me, but to my family, and to the memory I have of Charlie Collins," said Simonson, at a podium. "These are the epitome of fake news. A reporter, fishing for a story, coercing children at-the-time to give false reports about their adopted parents. Charlie Collins was a mentor to me and was a valuable servant of government. It is flat out wrong to level these accusations against a dead man, unable to defend himself."

"In the wake of the report, and the discovery of Price's body, Walters has come out further to say that Price's disappearance was related to his own investigation into the conspiracy, and she suspects it was part of the cover-up. The authorities have made no official statement, but this very morning, they took Speaker Simonson into custody."

The feed cuts to another video, this time of Simonson looking disheveled, his hands behind him in cuffs. A police officer marches him out of his home and pushes him into the back of a squad car. Simonson glances at the cameras, buts keeps his head down, trying to hide his face as much as possible.

"The story is still developing, but here at The Truth, we feel confident enough in our reporting to say that this is a clear false flag operation. The liberal media has created this conspiracy out of thin air, Diana Walters cover for a vast network of paid operatives, trying to undermine our government, and Adam Simonson."

Another pivot, John's eyes even harder now.

"And involving Leo in all of this. Leo Price was a friend of mine, integral to me working for The Truth, and I reluctantly took his position after his departure because I wanted to make sure the job was done right, like Leo would have done. And now they are attempting to sully his good standing. Leo was corrupted, leading to erratic behavior, and then killed, his body held until the proper moment, as to frame Adam Simonson."

John's eyes looked down for a second, struggling, and then back up to the camera.

"It is reprehensible, and says a lot about how far the liberals are willing to go, and we here at The Truth will not stand for it."

"And now it's time for a break with a word from our sponsors," said John, a slow gentle smile on his face.

.

John retreated to his office, the program over. Everyone

knew to leave him alone until he decompressed. Except for Warren, who was in there like a bolt of lightning, two minutes after John sat down. His head hurt, and he did not want to talk to Warren today.

"Good show again, John," said Warren. "You're killing it."

"Thanks," he said. "The numbers been all right?" He asked Warren as if John didn't know, as if he didn't wait for the results with bated breath.

"Ratings have been great," said Warren. "People are eating up the Price/Collins/Simonson story. It's the biggest news in years, and we've got every angle covered."

Warren's eyes stayed glued to his clipboard, and John studied Warren. Word went around, as hard as it sometimes was. John had heard about Warren's conversations with Leo, leading up to his leaving The Truth. He had learned about Leo trying to pursue an investigation, something big, and Warren shooting him down, over and over again.

He hadn't liked Leo. He had respected him, but Leo was a loud asshole, who never backed down, no matter how wrong he was. But John hadn't wanted him dead. And now, hosting the show for a month—he understood Leo's behavior a little bit better.

"How did Leo die, Warren?" asked John.

Warren's eyes looked up, over the edge of his glasses.

"Why are you asking me that?" asked Warren.

"Because he sure as hell wasn't killed by the liberal media," said John.

Warren dropped his clipboard to his waist, and stared at John.

"I will have this conversation one time, John," said Warren. "And one time only. I made mistakes with Leo. I should have been more honest with him. I might have been able to control the situation better. But you saw what happened. Leo followed a case, and it killed him. I don't know more than that. And I'll tell you what I told him. That we are not interested in the truth here. We're interested in a story. They might sometimes coincide. But if you want to be a reporter, a journalist, go somewhere else. And do it now. And be aware that you could end up like Leo. Do you understand?"

"I understand," said John. "I don't intend to leave."

"Neither did Leo," said Warren. "We can talk tomorrow's show in the morning. Take care of yourself."

Warren left without a glance back.

John walked over to the bar. John didn't drink. He had never been a big drinker, even in college. He poured himself a scotch now, with a single ice cube.

He sipped on it, grimacing at the taste. He sometimes could feel Leo still here. He had occupied the space for eight years. He had led the show from it. It had been a home away from home for him.

John didn't believe in ghosts, and he dismissed the idea that he felt Leo around him. It was an overactive imagination. He was imagining that feeling because of Leo's death. If Leo was alive and well at some other network, he wouldn't think about auras or spirits.

It was his imagination.

He drank more, knowing his driver would take him home, drunk or not. If you asked John why he drank, he would have said it was the stress building up, of being the face of something like The Truth. He knew of Leo's reputation as a drinker, and only now was understanding it.

He wouldn't mention the nightmares. He didn't remember them at first, but they stuck around longer and longer in the mornings, lingering at the edges of his memory, sometimes intruding on his vision, as he stumbled in his bedroom.

In the nightmares, he saw Leo die. Strangled to death, in a warehouse. But that wasn't what stayed with him.

It was her eyes.

John didn't see them at first. He was watching Leo. Then he noticed the eyes, wide, stark, lidless orbs that peered at him from the darkness. And then he would see the woman they belonged to, her skin pale, her body elongating as he stared. She would stare at him, from the shadows, as Leo struggled. And then she would come toward him.

She would come toward him, and she would scream, and he would hear everything she knew.

Acknowledgments

Thank you to my wife Kim, for her patience and support, and my team of beta readers: Andrew, Matt, Megan, Yousef. And thank you for reading.

About the Author

Robbie Dorman believes in horror. Truth is his second novel. When not writing, he's podcasting, playing video games, or petting cats. He lives in Texas with his wife, Kim.

You can follow Robbie on Twitter @robbiedorman

His website is robbiedorman.com

Subscribe to his newsletter at robbiedorman.com/newsletter

Enjoy Truth?

Sign up here to be notified about Robbie's next novel!

robbiedorman.com/newsletter

www.ingramcontent.com/pod-product-compliance
Lightning Source LLC
Chambersburg PA
CBHW050259110726
47898CB00007B/2468